Carnaval Fever

Carnaval Fever

a novel

Yuliana Ortiz Ruano

translated from the Spanish by
Madeleine Arenivar

Soft Skull   New York

This is a work of fiction. All of the characters, organizations, and events portrayed in this novel are either products of the author's imagination or are used fictitiously.

Copyright © 2025 by Yuliana Ortiz Ruano
Translation copyright © 2025 by Madeleine Arenivar

All rights reserved under domestic and international copyright. Outside of fair use (such as quoting within a book review), no part of this publication may be reproduced, stored in a retrieval system, or transmitted in any form or by any means, electronic, mechanical, photocopying, recording, or otherwise, without the written permission of the publisher. Additionally, no part of this book may be used or reproduced in any manner for the purpose of training artificial intelligence technologies or systems. For permissions, please contact the publisher.

First Soft Skull edition: 2025

Library of Congress Cataloging-in-Publication Data
Names: Ortiz Ruano, Yuliana, 1992- author | Arenivar, Madeleine translator
Title: Carnaval fever : a novel / Yuliana Ortiz Ruano ; translated from the Spanish by Madeleine Arenivar.
Other titles: Fiebre de carnaval. English
Description: New York : Soft Skull, 2025.
Identifiers: LCCN 2025020612 | ISBN 9781593768096 hardcover | ISBN 9781593768102 ebook
Subjects: LCSH: Ecuador—Fiction | LCGFT: Novels
Classification: LCC PQ8220.425.R88 F5413 2025 | DDC 863/.7—dc23/eng/20250509
LC record available at https://lccn.loc.gov/2025020612

Jacket design and illustration by Victoria Maxfield
Book design by tracy danes

Soft Skull Press
New York, NY
www.softskull.com

Printed in the United States of America

1 3 5 7 9 10 8 6 4 2

He'd come to our house in Santo Domingo in a busted-up taxi and the gifts he had brought us were small things... I didn't know what to make of him. A father is a hard thing to compass.

> Junot Díaz, *This Is How You Lose Her*

It turns out that sometimes, faced with what has to be said, words seem to soften and hang, flaccid and dripping saliva like the tongues of the hanged.

> Severo Sarduy, *Firefly*, translated by Mark Fried

Contents

1. Leave it all on the floor — 3
2. México and Cartagena — 21
3. Skinny pain-in-the-neck — 27
4. Caleñita — 45
5. Five-headed monster — 61
6. Voluntad de Dios — 69
7. An inflatable papi — 75
8. Mami Checho is water — 85
9. Chamber pot — 101
10. Little dugout canoe — 117
11. Fever — 129
12. Sabrosura — 139
13. Whiskey — 159
14. Mama Doma — 161
15. Whales — 171
16. Flor de verano — 183

Song list — 191

Carnaval Fever

1.

Leave it all on the floor

Ñaño Jota died, he kick off, my Papi Manuel told me when he came to pick me up from school and take me to the wake. I was nervous all day, could feel the delirium sprouting from the mouth of my stomach up to my tongue, a mass of slime creeping up and down, heralding something heavy. Heavy like the voice of the rag-and-bone men who come up to the neighborhood sometimes, yelling through their hoarse loudspeakers: annnyyyy oollll' iroooon, annyyy scrap metal, raaag aaan' boooone!

Heavy, like my Mami Nela saying that when Ñaña Marilú died, she started up like she'd had a bucket of cold water thrown in her mug. That's how death shows up, mijita. Something similar was happening in my young body, a mass coming up announcing something that couldn't be scraped off the tongue and turned into words.

Papi Manuel parked his old Ford close to the curb where I always sit to wait for him. From a long way off I could hear the sound of that beast getting closer, an erratic rumble against a background of Lavoe at full volume. For Papi Manuel, the rumble of that machine, heralding its own death, wasn't enough; he had to dampen the roar of that noise with the honeyed voice of Héctor Lavoe, who shared his name, gasping loudly out of the beat-up speaker like a death rattle.

My papi was loaded. He always likes his whiskeys, but this time he was loaded like people only get at a wake. Yeah, that's it, Ñaño Jota died, the mass said to me, and it started rising now like a stone rolling uphill along the bones of my chest. My papi had on a black collared shirt with shiny white buttons, black pants held up with a belt, white canvas sneakers with a brown patch, like shit, on the top near the laces. The older girls who were standing around said, look at that daddy, he so fine. That made me mad and I went over so they wouldn't mess with him. Mami Nela was right when she said the girls these days come out hot from the factory.

Mijita, your Ñaño Jota... mijita, your Ñañito Jota kick off. Even now, his voice rising up from the depths of his throat, hoarse from the drink, this papi can't give the news without a stupid little giggle. Like the giggle of La Lupe in that song he puts on sometimes on Sunday nights, the song that says this fever isn't new. It started a long time ago. And then she laughs out of nowhere, like a crazy person. My Papi Manuel also laughs out of nowhere, just like his idols, always just when he shouldn't. What're you laughing for, what's the matter with you? I pressed myself against his shirt, gagging on a thick cry, and inhaled the heavy funk of drink, tobacco, and perfume of this papi.

I felt him sob gently behind his brown glasses, and I lifted my head to see tears rolling down his face into his mustache. Papi Manuel's head looks like an upside-down light bulb, but with a long-haired Afro full of nice, tight curls. Mami Checho doesn't like Papi Manuel's hair, but I think it's pretty.

My Papi Manuel is a skinny guy, so skinny that sometimes you can see the bones poking out under his throat. But he's strong, strong enough to lift the gas tanks for cooking and to punch out the thieves who tried to make off with the truck that one time. My Mami Checho doesn't like the truck either, she's always telling him to sell that old rattle already, that it's a disgrace. But my papi adores that truck, he says to her, mi reina, you can't fight love.

Like almost everybody in this house, Papi Manuel

is known for his good smell. The women in my house all smell so good and are so neat that sometimes I look at myself in the mirror over my Mami Nela's dresser and I ask myself if I'm really a woman. I stink, a lot. My Mami Checho, since she birthed me, she always sends me back to wash again even when I've just come out of the shower. Scrubs my underarms in a desperate rage, sometimes her and my Papi Manuel together.

The two of them scrubbing away at my underarms so much that after the bath they throb, and even then they start to stink again. Ay and this girl, why she still smell like a pig? She sick or she just don't know how to wash? They blame themselves for the funk of my body as they scrub me in the cold shower and sometimes I cry. Not because it hurts but from the shame, because Mami Nela always says that women don't smell bad like that and what's the matter with the girl?

And I'm still there smelling like rotten onions and cat piss in the middle of the bustle of the gaggle of women who live in my Mami Nela's house–who isn't my mami who gave birth to me but my grandma, a word that she hates.

My Papi Manuel hoisted me up into the truck to take me to the house where they were holding the wake for Ñaño Jota. I buried myself in the red leather seat, the only thing in this car my papi had spent any money on. But instead of giving the truck back its dignity, as he claimed, it gave it the look of a cheap whorehouse, ready for the putas to dance. I'd never seen a whorehouse in my life, but that's what my Mami Nela hollered when she saw Papi Manuel coming back from the shop, shouting with joy over his souped-up truck.

My Ñaño Jota was beautiful. His black skin shone as if he polished it every day before leaving the house, he had big white teeth like slices of coconut, and he had a different tone of voice for everybody, especially for the women. He always dressed in white and for that my Mami Nela asked him if he was a pimp or what. But he never cared much what she thought.

Every Saturday morning, while I was waiting to go out to play, I would watch Ñaño Jota come out of the bathroom into the backyard of Mami Nela's house with a white towel tied around his hips. Before he went to get dressed, he would take his white canvas sneakers, drench them with water, and sprinkle on soap or detergent, whatever was left there on the laundry sink where the ñañas washed the clothes. He would spread that all over the sneakers and then scrape at them with an old toothbrush; a swish-swish as he hummed some song by Vicente Fernández, waggling his eyebrows at me. When he could see his face in them, he would leave them on the bathroom roof to dry while he went to get dressed. T-shirt printed with flowers, usually red, black, or tiger stripes, white high-waisted pants with pleats emphasizing his package and his ass, and a white belt to hold in the skin of his stomach. Then he would scrape over the tight curls on his head with a tiny little comb like the ones you use to find lice, and go out through the back of the house, through the secret exit, slipping through the fence like a black panther.

I'd never seen a panther in real life either, but that was what I thought when I saw him swing himself through, sucking in his voluptuous body to slip through the barbed wire without a sound. From the branch of the guava tree I would watch, blinded by the whiteness of his sneakers and his pants, spotless. And although I'd have sworn he brushed against the wire, nothing scratched Ñaño Jota, nothing could touch him.

When I was three years old, Ñaño Jota—who wasn't my brother either but the brother of my Mami Checho—told me that it was time I learned to dance. He took me with his rough, black hands to the center of the dance floor: the parlor, on any other day, but today with the furniture arranged so that there was space for the whole family. For all the dancers. That year, like every year, Carnaval started in December. Because Carnaval isn't only February and the days it says on the calendar, but any party that goes all night long. And in Esmeraldas, where the pounding heat never lets up for a second, a nice spray or bucket of water hit you and you might even give thanks.

> So, mija
> Like this: forward, backward, mijita,
> and your waist,
> yes, and the hips,
> See... what's wrong, you shy?
> Nuh-uh, don't be shy, mija,
> one and two
> and like this
> and to the side
> and over here
> and two.

From the big radio sounded the voices of Los Van Van singing "Aquí el que baila gana."

My Ñaño Jota said that dancing is just listening with your hips, mija, nothing more, your feet just move by themselves, look.

> It's not rocket science, mija: let's go
> and two and two

and two and like that.
Yes,
to the front, mija,
don't be shy, shyness don't get you nowhere.
And move that waist, mija, like this,
more, like I do it.
Look, mija, no,
like this and
to the back
and to the front
and eh eh eh eh
eeeehhhhso.

One day before Carnaval, the ñañas—who aren't really my sisters but the sisters of my Mami Checho, but how awful the word *tía*, and anyway they are young and not a bunch of old harpies—did my hair like a cluster of spiders. They made me my Carnaval braids sitting around on the wooden chairs from the dining set while I sat in the middle on the wooden floor. I watched the dogs pass by, and the hours, I started to get sleepy, and they still kept on braiding. They doused our hair with water and hair oil, untangled the whole thing before starting to braid, and once they started the do they wouldn't stop for the end of the world.

My Mami Checho doesn't like them to put colorful

balls on the ends of the braids because it looks tacky. Mija, you're not gonna go around looking like those trashy girls from up the hill in the Guacharaca. Instead they just tied them up with little black elastics, so the braids wouldn't unwind. Since my hair is so long and thick, sometimes I would fall asleep while they kept braiding. They would always start with a little tuft from the bottom of my head, divide it into three strands, and twist it up. All this with breaks for hot cocoa and bread, pineapple juice and water to refresh us, laughing and praising my hair until just after dawn they finished the braiding on the very top of my head.

Mija, there's nothing like a woman with good hair, I swear. When you grow up, you gon' make a clean sweep. If you ever decide to cut your hair, mija, you give it to me to make an extension. Your hair would look pretty straightened too, but when you're bigger, cuz that chemical burns the scalp and you little still.

Nervous, and with my braids all sweaty, I took my first salsa steps to the joy of my Papi Manuel and the alarm of my Mami Checho. The whole neighborhood partied all night. I still couldn't party all night, but I heard the beat from my room. And as the hours passed, from the hills the music rose up even louder. The song of the moment was "La suegra voladora," by El Sayayín, a hard Colombian champeta that brayed out through the neighborhood, and two songs by Grupo Saboreo: "La arrechera" and "La vamo a tumbar." When that chorus of "La vamo a tumbar" started up, the people went crazy and it was jumping and jumping on the wooden floorboards. Leave it all on the floor.

Whenever I heard those lyrics, I was possessed by La Lupe's giggle, because I had never heard anything so ridiculous as that song. How could that singer be happy they were gonna tear his house down? The house he worked so hard to build, like it says in the lyrics. The song starts with a sound like birds squawking but my Papi Manuel explained to me, laughing, that they were Colombian gaitas and not animals, and then the voice comes in singing about that house, built with hard work and a floor of guayacán. But then the gaitas come back and that booming voice yells, surely and firmly, getting right into your backbone, that today they gon' tear that house down.

And the people would go into some kind of trance, jumping around, the walls vibrating, that house was gonna get torn down to the beat of Grupo Saboreo, no matter what. I would sit on the couch and imagine the floorboards collapsing, the frames with pictures of Mama Doma and the knickknacks falling on top of everyone, still continuing their feverish dance under the rubble of that big house, of cement and wood, with twelve bedrooms, a big front porch full of plants, and a backyard dense with mango, guava, and chirimoya trees. I imagined the party going on under the rubble, sliding through the passageway, beyond the porch, and destroying the cistern, the only cistern in the neighborhood, built by my Papi Chelo—who's not my papi who made me but the papi who made my Mami Checho—and supplying the whole neighborhood with water.

The one who liked that song the most was Ñaña Catucha—who isn't my ñaña either but the ñaña of my Mami Nela. Ñaña Catucha loves to party. To dance that song she would kick off her sandals and her thick, black feet would sweep over the wooden boards polished with creosote, shining like the color of her skin. And how the ñañerío jumped, the gaggle of women. Their skirts swung around, and their manes of hair, while the men were all falling off the couches from laughing so hard.

After those days of Carnaval when I learned to really dance, to make my bony little body sweat like a wild horse, nobody could stop me. I danced in the bath, to salsa or that song by El Sayayín, "La suegra voladora," that song that my Mami Checho hated. My Papi Manuel had taught me to capture the music from the radio on a cassette tape so I could hear it any time I wanted, but whenever I put that cassette on, my mami would say, for crying out loud, turn that shit off, that it made all the hairs on her arms stand on end. And I couldn't understand why she didn't like it or even giggle about it a little.

I adored that slow voice slinking out of the speaker and the bom bom, bom bom bom bom, bom bom of the track that my Papi Manuel grumbled the Black Colombians had stolen from the Jamaicans. I liked to see everyone strutting the champeta across the floor. It made me laugh. I loved to see Noris and the other girls who cleaned the house throwing themselves on top of one another, chorusing, ya le cogí el maní, le cogí el maní ní, ya le cogí el maní, le cogí el maní.

Ñaño Jota also loved to see me learn songs by memory: mija, you have a good ear, let's hear it, sing something, come over here and sing for me a little. And I would unfurl my shrill little voice to imitate El Sayayín, riding on that little flying cloud, just like the song says.

When no one was watching me, I danced through breakfast; I got out of bed in the morning already moving my feet and hips.

Later, when many months had passed and Ñaño Jota suddenly thinned down as if something invisible were sucking his blood, his cheeks covered with grayish patches, and his eyes sunk in like two lakes filmed with oil spills, I understood that dancing was also his way of making himself well. A forgetting in which the body sweats so much it's no longer rickety, bedridden, and scrawny. Sweats so much it sweats the sickness out, for a little bit at least, that's why he had to dance so much and every weekend. And even more on Sundays, to stick the health in the body all week and keep the sickness out.

All the women in the neighborhood just died for him. They always came looking for him, even once he was married and had kids.

Women came from Pimampiro, from Santa Rosa, Vuelta Larga, and even from Quito. Women from Limones and Tumaco. Fat women wearing tight dresses, their eyebrows shaved off and in the empty space of the destroyed brow, a shaky line drawn with a brown or black pencil. Skinny women with big teeth and big-assed women with long braids who did my hair and brought me presents. Who danced as well as he did in the Carnaval parties, when his wife would go back to her sisters' neighborhood.

Even with all the dancing, my uncle died young and handsome, although thinner and with those strange patches all over his face and on the roof of his mouth, which I could see because that plague hadn't taken away any of his height. When his fever didn't go down no more and he couldn't get out of bed, I asked my Mami Nela what was wrong with the ñaño, that I had a right to know. But she pretended not to hear me and just kept on with what she was doing.

I was eight years old when he kicked off and I wasn't very tall yet. That's why I could see the roof of his mouth all white, like the inside of the young coconuts that Papi Chelo brings from his ranch up on the island that has our name, the Tolita de los Ruano. Papi Chelo is pale, tall, and sinewy; he stands out against the Black flock in this house, even against his daughters, who are not pale but neither are they black, a mixture closer to caramel than to chocolate. But mercy on anyone who tells them they aren't Black. BLACKITY-BLACK, they shout.

Papi Chelo has a nose like a toucan beak that all us women have inherited, as if it had been traced directly onto our mugs. He would often say, proudly and in his funny accent from the northern islands, closer to Colombia than to Ecuador, that he was the first man of his last name to have made it with a Black. There were always stifled giggles around the dining table after that speech. Papi Chelo is sweet to me, but he didn't like Ñaño Jota much. Sometimes they yelled at each other and even smacked each other around in the yard. They never let me see but I knew what was going on, I'm not deaf.

All of this was going round in my head as we were driving to the wake, my face pressed into the blindingly red leather seats of the old Ford. I remembered Ñaño Jota talking to the girls from the neighborhood in the passageway when they came by, supposedly to get water, but really just to kiss, dance with him, or go down into the cistern together and close the top, as if the cistern were a pool. Sometimes I thought they would come out drowned, but they always came out dripping wet and screeching as if the cistern were the Las Palmas beach.

I started to feel a terrible fear and an endless gratitude, a strange mixture that was eating up my body, like the body of the voice that comes out of kids when they recite the poem "Barrio Caliente is burning, burning is Barrio Caliente." I was burning up just like when that neighborhood turned to ash, starting at my toenails: the little hairs on my big toe, my socks with the school logo on them, my brown leather shoes, the skin and the long hairs on my shins. My knees boiled and disintegrated. The flames licked up my thighs, my backbone, my coochie, the burning sensation lingering in my hips. I felt the skin covering my muscles melting like chewing gum against the seats, red as the allure of the frigate birds, of that beast driving me along. Crying curled there in the passenger-seat window, I imagined Ñaño Jota dancing a diabolical rumba like the flames of Barrio Caliente in the truck bed.

I gave way to a horrible frenzy that only comes on me when my temperature goes up and I start to run through the whole house like a bitch in heat, raving, Mami Nela tells me. It wasn't my mouth, but the fever, the fever that didn't start now but a long time ago, that spoke for me. I told my papi to stop the car and put on some salsa, some good salsa for dancing, please.

Be serious, mijita.

AIDS, your Ñaño Jota died from AIDS. Mijita, pordios, you don't celebrate something like that. And he let out his little giggle, like a drunken rat, which only turned up the heat of my insistence. When my Papi Manuel laughs like that, I know that if I just let loose he'll do whatever I want. I screamed and begged without stopping for breath, like a guacharaca bird. Finally he gave in.

We parked the truck going up Calle Montúfar, seven blocks from our neighborhood.

The neighborhood of Calle Montúfar is always full of dirty kids running around with no shoes on. On the weekends, like in any Esmeraldeñan neighborhood, the residents bring out their speakers and sit on the curb to sip their whiskey, close the street to play ball dodging the cars, the trucks, and the bus that has already taken more than one little kid. We stopped right next to the corner that takes us to Calle México. My Papi Manuel opened the doors of the truck and took a packet of cigarettes out of the glove box. I got down in a daze as the cowbell that announces the mythical question of "Aquí el que baila gana" rang out at high volume, asking, what's happening here, eh?

Forward, backward, like this, mijita
move your waist,
and the hips,
one and two like this
and to the side
to the front
and one and two and two.

And what had happened here? My Ñaño Jota had been taken by something called AIDS, and I didn't know what it meant, like almost everything around me. Opaque to my confused little head. I started dancing right there, in my school uniform and with my eyes shut, listening to my Papi Manuel's nervous giggles as he sat down in the passenger seat, blowing out smoke and watching me with a crazed look on his face.

People came running over to the Ford to the rhythm of the music, applauding all together like seals, stomping their feet like a bunch of dumb clowns, because any stupid shit is a big event in that neighborhood where nothing ever happens, other than a kid smashed up, once in a while, by the number 2 line of the Las Palmas bus.

2.

México and Cartagena

Mami Nela's house is in the middle of two neighborhoods, serious business. Just up the street from the Immaculate Heart of Mary school, and when I say serious business, it's that there's like a transparent curtain between them and us, a skinny line that divides the good from the bad. A division that rises up with the words: oooh baby girl, you don't have nothing to do up the street; or, yuyi, no mi amor, you only go out with us and never, mi amor, seriously, don't be the kind of girl who hangs out in those neighborhoods.

And me always fighting the urge to ask why, if we're all here together, we are seemingly the good ones and those people up the street, on the right and the left, are the bad ones. We live at México and Cartagena, in the middle, between two neighborhoods: the one on the left, Guacharaca, and the one on the right, 20 de Noviembre. Sometimes I would daydream that, in reality, it was us in the middle who were the sonofabitches. That it was us the police chased with gunshots, like I once saw my Papi Chelo shoot at a pig before roasting it out on the ranch, out there on the island where we were born. That it was in our faces that bus doors banged closed and taxi drivers told us to get out, when we said the name of our neighborhood. But it wasn't that way. There's something heavy that stretches between those two hills that shelter us, something that can't be named, leaving us sandwiched between a bunch of thugs and hooligans.

Sometimes when I would wear short shorts, the girls who cleaned our house would tell me to take those off immediately! That my Mami Checho was gonna ask them why were they dressing me like the trash from Guacharaca? Sometimes the same girls would insult each other by saying that one was from Guacharaca or 20 de Noviembre—or even worse, from Isla Piedá. But I didn't understand what was the difference between them and us, what gave to us the veil of good girls and to them the label of putas, or fast, which is what Mami

Nela would say when I was there and she didn't want me to learn bad words.

She would say, those vulgar girls, they fast when they see a man, no? But I knew that inside that word, like when you open an avocado just at five o'clock and sprinkle in sugar, mash it up, and eat it as the sun is setting and the people are coming home to roost, was the word *puta*, like a badly kept secret. Puta, the perfect pit resting in the middle of the avocado.

Our house, or really, Mami Nela's house, where I've lived since I was born, is so big and so strange that nobody can deny its beauty: two entire floors, with twelve bedrooms all full of heavy polished wooden beds and wispy yellow, white, or pink mosquito nets; a giant parlor also full of heavy wooden furniture and strange trinkets, mostly porcelain dolls given as souvenirs in some baptism or quinceañera, all enclosed in glass and wood display cases, always clean, always polished to a shine by Noris's hands. Noris is one of the girls who clean the house. The girls are always many, new, and different. But Noris has crossed the threshold of cleaning girl and is like family now, even though she's always cooking and washing things, she's part of the family, that's what they say.

What's strangest to me about the inside of the house is not the furniture, or the caged trinkets, or the rugs that Mami Nela hooks on the weekends to place under the trinkets, or the red rotary phone that I have never seen used. I'm not afraid of the wood-paneled ceiling or the gold lamps that hang down like bats from the roof beams, not at all of the vinyl-coated wallpaper with squiggly lines that makes me dizzy sometimes. I'm not afraid of the windows in the bedrooms, or the ones in the parlor that open onto the porch filled with plants: aloe, beebrush, mint, lime, kalanchoe, escancel, rue, paico, ambrosia, matico, plantain, and chickweed, which Mami Nela uses to make her cures, to switch anyone who comes to her with espanto or the evil eye. That all seems normal to me, but what always fascinates me is the imposing painting of Mama Doma that rests on the main sideboard in the parlor.

The portrait of Mama Doma follows me with a penetrating gaze to any corner of the room. Sometimes, to test it, I come through the door that opens at the top of the outside stairs, run across the room, and throw myself under the sideboard. I count one, two, three, open my eyes and even there her hard, dark eyes like little palm seeds are watching me tensely. There is an invisible line that separates fear from respect, like the line that makes some good and others bad. That line is like a cord you can jump rope with and be on both sides, sometimes on the good side and other times on whatever you got, wherever your feet fell, left or right.

That's how I feel when Mami Nela tells me about God. There's a line that makes me fear Him, and on the other side respect Him. That feeling expands through my bones, beats in my blood, in the same way when Mami Checho tells me excitedly the story of how Mama Doma saved her life. Mami Nela's parlor is the eyes of Mama Doma, the woman who gave birth to Mami Nela, that is to say, the woman who gave birth to us all. Those eyes on the furniture, the coffee table full of shiny black elephants that bring luck. Mama Doma's eyes running over the walls and the side tables full of picture frames in every corner. At every turn a little table of glass and wood covered in smiling images of my ñañas, Papi Chelo, a graduation of some extended-family uncle who I'll never meet, and other unfamiliar faces. Mama Doma's eyes on our bodies as we eat all together around the dining table. Or really, as we women eat all together around the dining table, because the papis are never there. There are Mama Doma's eyes, watching creepingly every one of my steps. I'm afraid to creak the wooden floorboards when I walk, because I can feel on the bones of my neck the gaze of the Midwife Doma, which is at the same time the gaze of God on my body.

The gaze of a Black goddess, blackity-black, over every thing.

3.

Skinny pain-in-the-neck

I spend all day perched up in a tree in Mami Nela's backyard, talking to the guavas. Really, I'm talking more to the worms that live inside the guavas. I ask them how they got all that way to the dusty pink heart of the fruit, how is it possible there is a life beating inside a guava, with no hole on the outside, no door to enter. As soon as I'm done chatting, I desperately shove a wormy guava in my mouth and it becomes mine. Inside, I imagine the brief life of the worms: a chalky invertebrate life that now becomes part of my bony girl stomach. I stuff myself; sometimes I don't even want lunch, and then the problems start.

Eat, mija, you look like I could break you in half, mamita. Mija, eat before it gets cold, a skinny woman, too skinny, is a sick woman, mija. Do you want people to call out you rickety in the street? No, mija, then you gotta eat. But I don't want to eat, I feel sick. I think about the animals with no bones chopped up into little pieces inside my body, running all through me, dissolving into my liquids, my blood. I see them come out of my coochie like when the neighbor Remberto's dog gave birth near our yard, and perched like always in one or another of the trees, I witnessed the miracle of becoming a dog by splitting open the body of your mother.

The only one that can convince me to eat is my Ñaña Rita, one of the younger sisters of Mami Checho. They call her the skinny pain-in-the-neck, because she's thin and always getting in trouble. She has a face out of a black-and-white magazine, eyes too large and a mouth that's too small. She's always hot-blooded but not with me; with me she's all giggles and hairdos with colorful bows and feeding me soup and taking me out to eat with the boys who come calling for her. There are a lot of them, because Rita is the most beautiful of Mami Nela's daughters.

To me they are all equally beautiful, but I know that she is the most beautiful of the daughters because that's what they yell at her, the boys gathered on the street corners when we go walking by to the beach or the corner store. Lookit that beauty, the mos' beeyooteeful of Doña Nela's girls. Rita just clasps my hand tightly, closes up her face, and keeps walking, toughening her bones and tautening her skin, like the skin of an animal mounted on a drum to be beaten forever after, bringing forth the miracle of music.

What Ñaña Rita doesn't know is that angry she looks even more beautiful, and the boys' hollers just get louder on every corner. To me, a corner is that, a place for boys, for canvas sneakers and baggy T-shirts, bicycles and bucket hats, but above all for hollers and whistles. Only putas hang out on corners, Papi Chelo would mutter. So for me, the boys that hassle my Ñaña Rita must be putos. Putos! I yelled at them once, but my ñaña told me that little girls should never open their mouths to say dumb shit like that.

They don't let my Ñaña Rita go out much, because she is too pretty. When my Papi Chelo arrives from the ranch, he's always looking out for her. Rita, where are you going missy, no, come upstairs now. Rita, heat up my food and set the table. Mijita, you don't have permission to go down. Rita, come here, I'm talking to you. They shut up in the room and pretty soon Rita starts up with her yelling because they never let her go out and it makes her mad. That's why she takes me all over, because with me they do let her go out.

She tells me, Ainhoa, let's go get a drink and a hamburger with a friend at the park, mijita, ok? Go get dressed but don't say anything, I'll do the talking. You want to go to the park, right, mamita? The baby wants to go, Papi, I'll take her out to play a little bit and bring her right back. Or, yuyi, mijita, let's go down to the beach to eat some fried shrimp and fish, go get dressed. Ainhoa wants to go to the beach, Papi, I'll take her to swim and play a bit in the sand and we'll come right back.

And out we go in our teeny tiny skintight jean shorts, me with my purple semitransparent sunglasses and my big hair springing free, because Ñaña Rita is the only one who can do my hair. Everyone else just gives up, because, Jesus, this girl got a lot of hair. I know that my beauty, more like that of the bumpy green noni fruit than that of a human, can't compare to the dusty summer sunset in the eyes of my Ñaña Rita. A catlike energy knitting through her thin face. I can feel the tension in her smooth fingers gripping my bony hand as we walk by and the men's mouths gape open like a row of empty cowsheds.

We must look so strange, two rickety little women clinging to each other on the way to the beach.

My other ñañas, on the other hand, when they have to face up to the thick presence of my stinging-tentacled hair, just pull the braids harder, ripping through the tangles with the big-tooth comb. As soon as I see that huge comb, I know the torture is about to start and away I'm running to the guava tree. No one can get me down from there.

My Ñaña Rita, she knows how to comb my hair. First she douses it with shampoo, applies lots of conditioner, and combs through it slowly with her fingers, then she rinses it all out and applies plenty of oil and hair food. My long, thick hair shines, and I feel almost as pretty as her.

We go down Cartagena, our street, then all the way down México.

At the end of Calle México, in front of the Immaculate Heart of Mary school, the boyfriends are waiting.

Some of them come in cars, others on motorcycles or bicycles.

Some of them come on foot, with their bucket hats and their overalls, and they are, in general, the most good-looking. Beautiful boys the color of dulce de leche, grinning with happiness at the skinny cat, my Ñaña Rita.

They pick us up and we walk along chatting, because I can chatter like a sonofabitch.

I sit down in between Ñaña Rita and the boyfriend of the day, I stare right at them, and I ask them questions. How old are you? Really? I thought you would be older, and what's your name? Some of them answer me, others just stare at me weakly. They say to me, mija, don't you want to go play in the sand by yourself for a little bit? And me... well no... I want to stay here. But mijita, little girls don't talk like that, like an old lady. But my Ñaña Rita tells them to leave me alone, or she'll go, and that's that, she has her own money for her taxi back and to stop hassling the girl.

Rita is really skinny, rickety. So much so that sometimes she wears my shorts. So skinny that, when Papi Chelo is out at the ranch, and the boyfriends come by to ask for her, they say, buenas tardes, Doña Nela, is la flaca home? Or, buenas tardes, Señora Nela, is your daughter Bones in? And we all know that it's Rita they want, because she is the skinny pain-in-the-neck, the delicious Bones. La flaca rica.

They don't say that to Mami Nela, but to Rita herself, when I finally move over or get down to play. The boys think I can't hear them, but I hear everything. As my Papi Manuel says, little pitchers have big ears. I pretend not to hear and not to see their hands on my Ñaña Rita's legs, creeping up like the insects that crawl over you when you stay still for too long in the bush without moving or shaking them off.

Still, she hardly lets them touch her, or kiss her, or nothing. That's not fair, you said you wanted to go out to eat with me; well here I am, but you didn't say nothing else, she'll answer with her thin nasally voice, standing up, putting on her black sunglasses. Ok thanks, I'm going, let's go, mija.

We always eat well when we go out together. We go to the Porteñito café, and every time, I order the same thing: a hamburger and a blackberry-coconut milkshake. The boyfriends sometimes are shocked, because, man your niece, wow she can really eat, where she put all that food? Or, all that food go straight to your hair, mija. I just repeat my order, a large milkshake and a hamburger, and I chew it all serenely and they simply can't believe it.

Ñaña Rita just cackles and says, yeah, mija eats a lot, she's little and skinny but she's real smart and it's because this girl eats a lot. But it's not true, I don't eat a lot, I only gobble up the things I like: the guavas, and the hamburgers, for example. Or, yuyito can already read, when they write sappy notes on their napkins and I read them out loud, the dudes get spooked. I hold up the napkin and read:

> "Mi reina, how I would make you dream,
> in my arms you will be happy"

> or

> "Cuerpo a cuerpo" (the first verse painstakingly copied out word for word)

or

"Flaca,
I'm going crazy for your bones
I can't live another day without you,
come sleep with me,
mamita,
you won't ever regret it"

Caramba! And how old is this girl that she can already read?

Sometimes I ask my Ñaña Rita why those boys write such strange things, and she says, mamita, they're in love, you got to watch out for the love of men, mija, a man in love is capable of anything. Writing some crazy nonsense, shouting, threatening, stalking. God forbid, mija, God forbid a man fall in love with you.

Some of Ñaña Rita's boyfriends won't chat with me or even look at me, and then I start to go wild, like when the frenzy of the fever comes over me and I start to really go crazy. I go to sleep right there on the table of the hamburger stand under the neon lights, so that my ñaña will pick me up and take me home. I know that Ñaña Rita can't carry my weight, so I go to sleep hard so those boys will have to hoist me up on their shoulder, what, they think they can not talk to me?

Ñaña Rita doesn't really like any of her boyfriends. She just wants to go out to eat, see the city, visit the beach, or, as she says to me, take advantage of her youth.

Always when we get home Mami Nela grabs her and tells her to open her mouth, and she smells her. She smells her mouth and her hair and her neck. Always when we get home Mami Nela is sitting in the doorway, on the porch next to all the plants, her nostrils wide. They widen so much that sometimes I can see her brain.

Mami Nela always knows what's going on. Even though she wasn't there, she knows which boyfriend Ñaña Rita was with. You smell like man, Rita. Nobody gets by me. And she checks her all over. She looks at her legs and presses her fingers against her throat, to see if it throbs—if it throbs too much, it's because it's been touched by a man. My Mami Nela always smells all my ñañas and checks their throats, because, my daughters come down out of this house only to be married, carajo! she yells when the boyfriends come by asking for one of them, especially the skinny-cat pretty-boned Rita.

She also checks Noris and the other girls who clean house, who are many but always different because Mami Nela throws them out. Sends them back to the countryside for being stanky or warm. Heat I take only from my daughters, and that's cuz I know how to watch 'em, she chews to herself as she washes clothes in a brown tub on the laundry sink in the backyard.

I need to say that my Ñaña Rita is not warm. She's just too beautiful. She's so beautiful that sometimes it seems like she's wrapped in a kind of white gauze, as if there were a strange energy floating around her head. Like a saint. She's crazy beautiful, and the boys in the neighborhood bother her so much that it's better she not go out to do the shopping, they might seduce my baby away in the street. Ñaña Rita is so pretty that she's always getting in trouble without trying to. Like that late afternoon she was sent mariachis.

It was the first time we had ever heard those songs live, and we all went out excited to listen and applaud the men with wide hats and skinny black pants hugging their asses. Beaming, we all crowded onto the porch, as the blushing redheaded boy with brown freckles slowly walked toward us holding out a bouquet of flowers as red as his hair.

Really tall and really red, with freshly ironed black pants, a blue button-down shirt with white stripes down the sides, and a bucket hat that made him look like a bank teller from the neck down and a techno merengue singer from the neck up, as handsome as Sandy & Papo ready to sing.

The sun was going down behind the Guacharaca hill, giving everything an unusual red-orange tinge. We were all still there grinning when behind the red boy with a strange name, Rolon or Rolin or something, suddenly the sunbrowned nose of Papi Chelo appeared, with the sacks of young coconuts, the pineapples, and the men who carry the sacks for five sucres. He looked at all us women with disgust and spat on the ground near the mariachis. Buenas tardes, nice party, he rasped out as he went up the wooden stairs.

Since he didn't say nothing more, we all knew we were even more screwed. This must be the kind of fear of the love of men that Ñaña Rita had talked about. All the boys adored her and pined for her, would do anything to get her attention, stupid stuff and bad stuff too. I have never witnessed it myself but I can sense it, in the fear in the catlike eyes of my skinny-cat pain-in-the-neck ñaña.

The only thing I've seen myself is Papi Chelo's excessive love for her. A love that makes Rita turn red and cry, dragging herself along the floor when he shuts her in the bedroom. I get all jumpy but the other ñañas and Mami Nela just turn deaf ears and go start their sewing or prepare for their classes. Still I don't understand why she cries like that. Sometimes, when Papi Chelo comes from the ranch, Ñaña Rita doesn't want to come out of her room to see him at all. But he always goes in to take her out, to bring her out into his presence.

The love of men for their daughters is the most terrible, I soon learned.

That afternoon Ñaña Rita fell down trembling on the porch floor. The other ñañas felt like pissing themselves, but go up to the house, not a chance.

Brother, go on home now, I'm sorry but la flaca gets like this when she's excited, said Ñaña Antonia, the most intelligent of all the ñañas, who always knows how to talk her way out of any problem.

The party was over. The ñañas went up the stairs in single file, like they were going into the wake of a long-lost aunt, into the parlor where Papi Chelo was seated. Don Chelo, as the neighborhood calls him, Chelito, or Don Rúa—the ones who are most scared of him. Me, since nothing ever scares me, I'm always jumping all over him and he just laughs, but he is scary.

I know that because the whole ñañerío breaks out

in a cold sweat when he gets home. They walk around in silence, buenos días, Papi; buenas tardes, Papi; Papi, buenas noches, long faces staring fixedly at their feet. Shorts hidden away in the drawers with a false bottom, way in the back, and out come the long skirts, the loose T-shirts, hair pulled back in a plain bun and no messing around. But we always knew when he was coming, because Ñaña Catucha, who has a phone, would come and shout up that Don Chelo sent her to tell them to boil water for coffee, that he's on his way. Whenever that happened, the ñañas would run around like crazy tidying what was already tidy and washing what was already clean. The skin on the tips of their fingers ragged from chewing off their nails, waiting for Papi.

But this time no one gave the warning and the gaggle of ñañas was caught out, long legs sticking out of their itty-bitty jean shorts, thongs underneath. The ñañerío in crop tops showing off their belly buttons and a fringe of curls hanging down over their foreheads. The ñañerío telling Rolin or Rolon, the guy with the mariachis, that sure, ñaño, come on over to declare yourself to skinny Rita, no problem, because Papi's not at home.

And then, tugging on their too-small clothes, they went upstairs.

We went upstairs.

I also wanted to be there, to be present for the scolding.

My Papi Chelo called me: Ainhoa, come here, mija, sit here.

He lifted me up onto his lap and sniffed my hands.

Mijita, go tell your Ñaña Catucha that your Papi Chelo needs her to bathe you and keep you in her house awhile, that your Papi needs to talk to your ñañas, these girls are being vulgar, they're disrespecting this house. Immediately I sensed the blood and the brown horse whip hidden on the top shelf in the kitchen and I started to cry, because when I cry, the world stops and everyone gathers around trying to calm me down. Crying, I choked out, gulping on my snot, that I was already clean and that I didn't want to go to Ñaña Catucha's house, I wanted to stay here, Papito Chelo.

Just then my Mami Checho came up the stairs, dressed like always for her secretary job, and she immediately started trembling, tugging on her skirt, and trying to hide her nylon stockings.

And that's how you go to work, Checho?

Look, call Catucha for me, she needs to take this girl so I can fix this heat once and for all. He stood up and took off his belt, stretching it out from the buckle like a bolt of lightning, as if the belt weren't meant to hold up his pants at all but were a sword, a knife, some kind of weapon. Downstairs Ñaña Catucha was already waiting for me, chewing on nothing as if she were a cow, a strange tic she has. Come on, yuyito. She took me by the hand and led me to her house, not ten steps away from the passageway to Mami Nela's house.

She put some music on loud and I knew that my ñañas were getting beaten. I pissed myself, I cried until I was covered in snot, but she still wouldn't take me home. Later on my Mami Checho and my Papi Manuel came to get me. Their faces looked disjointed, like when you take a little crayon and scratch out a smiley face on a cement brick wall. An impossibly and unnecessarily happy grimace.

Thank you, Ñaña Catucha, for watching the baby, I'll take her now.

Except we didn't go back to Mami Nela's house but to the kebab stand at the beach that belongs to a friend of Papi Manuel's. Yuyito, we're going to move to a real pretty house just for us. Worried, I asked, which us? My ñañas and you? No, mijita, just us: Papi Manuel, me, and your little sister, who's a baby and needs her own space, just like you do. But in Mami Nela's house I have my own room. But here you'll have your own room too, mija, it'll be just us so we can be in peace.

I started to cry again, but silently this time, without knowing why. Maybe that was the beginning of my decline, this confusion that mixes me up like a head full of salad. Because after that I couldn't be a little girl anymore, although my size, my face, and my age were all little, but something was different. I didn't cry wildly anymore, or piss on the floor so they would listen to me, I just let the tears run down my cheeks dumbly. I fell asleep on a bench in the kebab restaurant, while Papi Manuel told his friends how brutal Papi Chelo was to my ñañas and that they couldn't turn a blind eye anymore.

That my Papi Manuel had grabbed Papi Chelo's belt right out of his hand and they almost get into it. That Papi Manuel had gotten home early by chance and found his wife there, scared and humiliated.

No sir, you can't go around beating people.

I'm from the country too, sonofabitch, and my father never whipped me, are we horses or what? God forbid, that man raises a hand against mija and I will rip him to pieces, my papi recounted as he drank and my Mami Checho just laughed softly. Maybe she was embarrassed; it's hard to tell what my mami feels because she's always changing energy, shifting moods and gestures. She's never the same.

Soon after that Papi Chelo stayed out at the ranch and didn't come back to Mami Nela's house. People say that he has another woman out there, but his presence is still visible throughout the house, in all the decorations on all the shelves. In his clothes that Mami Nela makes Noris wash and iron, even though no one uses them; in the place always set at the head of the table with a shiny clear plate and silverware freshly washed and polished.

We all knew he would return.

The terrible love of men, the terrible love of a father for his daughters always returns.

4.

Caleñita

Ñaña Antonia teaches me to memorize long, long poems to recite at family parties. Not only to recite them and make her look good but also to aggravate—for example, the poem "Remberto": I don't remember the whole thing, but it starts with that name, roaring. She says to me, mija, don't just say it, *feel* it. You have to feel the poem, mija, you can't just recite it like you were saying any old nonsense. No, mijita. And she stands up and raises her arms like a bad flamenco dancer. Waving her arms around to accentuate the words, until it seems like she's speaking another language. I imitate her, shout out the words. Bite into them, chew over them like she does, like I'm sucking down a big ripe mango, slow.

When that poem had nested in under my hair, she told me come on, mija, and she took me over to the fence that separates Mami Nela's garden from the neighbor's. She left me standing there and ran off into the house. From the window she whistled, ssssss, mija, now! And I started to shout:

REMBERTO
FROM BORBÓN YOU CAME
AMONG TOMBS AND BAMBOO

And then she went, ssssss, mija, louder!

And I kept on screaming out that poem like a dog giving birth, just to annoy the neighbor, Remberto. Remberto, the father of the red-haired boy named Rolin or Rolon. Remberto, the husband of a teacher at the school where my Mami Nela has taken me to practice writing since I was three, because she is also a teacher there.

Ñaña Antonia is the smart one. It's not that Mami Nela's other daughters aren't smart, but she is intelligence in flesh and blood, which basically means she can manage numbers and letters perfectly. They say she learned to add, multiply, and divide all in the same day, and at three years old she already knew how to read and write. Since she was ten she's made a little bit of money teaching math and counting to the littler neighbors, and sometimes to the bigger ones too, but now that she's becoming a young woman, my Mami Nela only lets her teach math to kids in elementary school or younger. Or those men will always be hitting on mija.

She always has a smile on her face, and a striking voice that rings out. Sometimes she seems like the spirit of a cunning old woman placed in the body of a little girl. She's beautiful, with her lush hair, her breasts like pears, and her brilliant smile, but she doesn't have an ass and that is a problem. The other ñañas are always harassing her, teasing her about her stick shape, because having an ass is almost required in this family, from what I understand you can be missing anything but an ass. They say to me, too, mijita, eat your plantains every day, so that even if you're skinny, you'll have a good ass. And I do it, but I'm still thin as a straw, like a girl cursed with the evil eye. The only thing thickening up on my body is my hair; my ass still hasn't sprouted.

But Ñaña Antonia's beauty fades once she starts to go on about romantic poems and songs by divas from Italy, Spain, or Argentina. The boys fidget, they start to yawn, to scratch their heads, and finally they run off when she mentions her book of poems. Maybe it's her way of escaping the terrible love of men, I don't know, but I love to listen to her.

I go into a kind of trance, the words carrying me away.

She has a green book, an anthology of Spanish and Mexican poems that she carries around like an icon, like a little image of a saint that you can't ever renounce or it will take away your parents, your children, and your dogs. It will take away your husband, the money you don't have. Leave you in the street. Ñaña Antonia has memorized all the poems in that book, and I'm well on the same path, because she helps me with my homework while my Mami Checho and my Papi Manuel are out at work to build the so-called new house where we will live happily ever after. Between each worksheet she calls me over, mija, come, let's read a little.

We lie in the hammock, her with the book and me with the excitement of getting to hear her voice biting into the poems. To me, Ñaña Antonia has a voice like the important men yelling on the radio. Like the men on the sports program that Papi Chelo would always listen to, dozing with his mouth open and his shirt up around his neck.

My Mami Checho can't stand that sports program. Whenever she gets home early from work and by accident someone has the radio on during the lunch hour, she runs desperately to turn it off. Don't turn that shit on, it brings up bad memories. Jesus, it makes me remember when they used to leave me out on the ranch, alone and with nothing to eat, waiting for my papi. Just leave the radio off, ok? If only we could have heard the voice of Ñaña Antonia coming out of the radio speaker, instead of those men who made my Mami Checho remember the ranch, and her hunger.

My Ñaña Antonia is like a well-behaved madwoman, mad and smart at the same time. A strange mixture that makes me bust out laughing. We always do our homework together, her homework and mine and the homework of some of the other kids in the neighborhood who come to ask her for help, because she is just too smart. But we also play strange, wild games that require a good memory and plenty of cunning.

On the ground floor of Mami Nela's house there is a large apartment, with two wood-framed picture windows that look out onto the porch. In that apartment lived a distant aunt, Tía Caleñita. And I call her tía and not ñaña because nobody knew her very well, or for very long. We only knew that she was a little bit blind because she was pretty old, and her husband, a military man much younger than her, stole her money. He stole all the income she got from some land she had in the north.

The husband looked like Charlie Chaplin but with a Colombian accent. The truth is I had to imagine the other half of his face, because whenever he arrived I could only see him through the little hole in the door of my room that looks out into the parlor. I saw him in profile, giving the rent money to my Mami Nela. He only paid the rent for the old lady's apartment and her food, the rest of the money he took away with him. But my Ñaña Antonia was convinced that she must have more money in there.

That's why Ñaña Antonia dressed up like a witch, because Caleñita loved witches.

She loved when the witches came by to read her tobacco leaves, make her herbal baths, and pray over her. My Ñaña Antonia was no fool; so that money wouldn't go to waste, she grabbed all the oldest and blackest clothes from my Mami Nela's dresser and piled them on. She draped herself in black scarves, one over her breasts and the other over her hips, and tied it all up with a piece of rope around her waist. She covered her face with a wine-red mosquito net and she lit up a cigar, one of those big ones my Mami Nela keeps in her dresser, too. She went out to the passageway, pretending she had just arrived, calling out in a feeble old lady's voice:

GOOOOD MOOOORNING
Is Señora Caleñita home?
Jesus and Mary have sent me to give you a message!
HAALLLLLOOOOOO
In the name of the Father
the chaste sacred
Virgin believer
Caleñita
HAALLLLLOOOOOO

She was banging on the door, yelling in a sinister, weird voice, like a deranged, feverish madwoman, and if I hadn't seen her transformation for myself, I would have gone running for the guava tree.

Tía Caleñita opened the door slowly, because she was sick, and once my Ñaña Antonia was inside, I came crawling in. First I drank down in one gulp the tía's half-finished carton of milk that was sitting on the table. Then I scurried like a rat along the edges of the room, while my Ñaña Antonia improvised an unintelligible prayer: a santamaría interrupted by shouting, choking, spitting alcohol in Caleñita's face, and coughing out that cigar smoke over her.

Convulsing, twisting around her body, and her eyes like the Devil was in her.

It was like:

Santamaría
Mother of God
Santamaría
Mother of God
Pray for us
Pray pray pray for us
Ay ay yaay
Yiyiyiiii
Feee verrrr
Ay ay ay.

And shouting and spitting that alcohol across Caleñita's whole face. And me, laid out on the floor, sliding like a shadow between the few pieces of furniture in that apartment, searching for the money hidden in an empty coconut oil bottle, painted black, always in a different spot. I grabbed ten, twenty, fifty, and a thousand sucres. My Ñaña Antonia wanted to bust out laughing seeing me chug so much milk, but she held it in and kept on with her role of witch, spraying that alcohol and coughing that cigar smoke. I stuffed the money into my Mickey Mouse underpants and went running out to the garden.

Tía Caleñita was so old she couldn't leave her room alone. Sometimes the ñañerío had to go in to help her walk about, to clean out the chamber pot full of shit and piss, to wash her ass. But she transformed whenever her husband arrived. When that Chaplin dude arrived, my Ñaña Antonia would tell me, Ainhoa, come here mija, let's go out to the yard to play at dancing. She would dress me up like the woman from the Pimpinela siblings duo or she would make up my eyes with black liner like Jeanette and she would make me mime the part of the sad girl. She was the man, and I was the woman, bawling out, "Olvídame y pega la vuelta," just go, forget about me, go back home.

And she did all this so that I wouldn't hear the shouting, the screwing. The pounding that Caleñita and her husband would give each other in that apartment down below. And my Ñaña Antonia would just bawl louder, that for two years she's been without love, trying to forget.

But even with all that bawling, I could hear with my big ears that they were screwing in that room.

That screwing was what kept my other ñañas from believing completely in Tía Caleñita's sickness.

I don't think she can be so sickly if she can eat her man so well, said my Ñaña Tita, the littlest of all the ñañas of my Mami Checho. And my Ñaña Antonia, you think? Doubting, because we went right in to rob her, me disguised as a bush rat and her as a witch, spitting and coughing.

No, Ñaña, wise up, a sick woman can't eat a man like that. When that sonofabitch comes, there's nothing we can do, no radio loud enough to hide that pounding, Ñaña Tita repeated over and over again, the littlest of all but the most peculiar, so strange, like a dried-up mummy in the sensual young body of a girl on the corner of México and Cartagena. Such a weirdo mummy that my Ñaña Antonia calls her the old lady. With a cackle, so she gets even madder, her face getting longer, older.

The poem that I most like to recite for my Ñaña Antonia is called "La tejedora de Ñandutí." I have no idea what a Ñandutí is, or where this lady is knitting all the time, but I like the rhythm, the bouncy chanting. It's the same with the songs on the radio that sometimes I record on cassettes, like my Papi Manuel taught me. There's one especially that sounds like the singer has a pile of fat slugs in his mouth, a big pile of slugs wiggling around in his mouth, as he brings the microphone right up close. And it sounds delicious.

They always play that zouk right at five in the afternoon, as the blazing sun starts to slip down behind the

Carnaval Fever

Guacharaca hill. I quit whatever I'm doing to turn on the radio and leave it all on the floor:

      Eh
    ya se que
    se la vi
u pag tu no me traguá
u pag le de pe ga mué
 a lo fema le li fe

pa le chi la matinal
y tua de que ni é fanal
su no li se fa na matal

  marg shon tal
 a casa te tutu ni
e vig meme tu tu nie
ca gas te ma con ti nue
o mañetas para comé

ti du vie leg ma fe
a lo teg ma lelife
   conchinie

shi mo to do no
 da la passió

Yuliana Ortiz Ruano

e yo tu ta fabuló
yo no fo
su sa si ma

chei me go
supeg a mog
o tu tie ma su blié

tu le tocá
qui no pasa si grei

ia mato na festa la vi
ya no sex o sí

basifonki
se bom

ba sifonki
se bom bom bom

basifonki
se bom

ba sifonki
se bom bom bom

Carnaval Fever

basifonki
se bom

ba sifonki
se bom bom bom

basifonki
se bom

ba sifonki
se bom bom bom

fruydalapassion fruydalapassion

I turn the volume all the way up and my ñañas make a conga line around me and

basifonki sebom
basifonki
se bombombom

My Ñaña Antonia, the smartest madwoman, she sure knows how to move. Everything she does comes out perfect. She can salsa, lambada, and even do schoolwork, an intelligence mixed with a heat and a smolder, a well-rounded intelligence:

basifonki sebom
basifonki
se bombombom

basifonki sebom
basifonki
se bombombom

It turns out that Tía Caleñita has a daughter, whose name is Goreti. That's what she said when she arrived out of nowhere to get the tía and take her away. She was unusually tall; it was the first time I saw a woman taller than my Papi Manuel, and she wasn't embarrassed to wear her tightly curling hair loose, you could tell there wasn't a drop of straightener in that thicket of hair. She wore bell-bottoms and a loose white shirt, and she wasn't wearing any bra. It took my breath away to glimpse the blackness of her nipples, revealed by the light shining through her clothes. I also fell in love with her green canvas shoes, lace-ups with white soles. I couldn't resist squatting down to look at them closer. They're called Converse, she told me with a smile, extending her hand to lift me from the floor and kiss my cheek. Her teeth were precious, they looked like they had been carved out of the whitest coconut meat and placed there behind her lips. Her eyes were almond shaped and she smelled like a mix of flowers and herbs, nothing like the odor of garlic and onions permanently steeped into the fingernails of my ñañas and Noris.

Goreti had managed to get an Italian husband and she lived with him in Europe, that's why she had a singsong accent and she couldn't pronounce her *r*'s correctly.

At first my Mami Nela wasn't sure if she should let her take Tía Caleñita or not, because, that girl has a crazy face, mija, I don't trust her. Mija, Goreti, you said your name was Goreti, right? We're taking good care of Caleña here, are you sure you want to take her away? But I had heard in a whispered conversation, like all the conversations my Mami Nela had with the ñañerío, that to rent out Caleña's room was gonna be a pain in the neck, mijas, please no, Jesus.

In the end, she took Tía Caleñita away. So that man will leave off robbing her, Tía, how could you let this happen, Tía? It's unheard of, it's criminal, Tía, she shouted, crying and shaking her loose hair around like the wind among the leaves, in those Converse shoes, which I dreamed about for several months until the Goreti effect faded. The new cousin, and I call her cousin and not ñaña, because that was the first time we saw her and I knew it would be the last.

5.

Five-headed monster

So, are they your sisters?

No.

So then why do you call them your ñañas?

Because they're my ñañas, don't you have ñañas?

My ñañas are my sisters, not my aunts. And your Mami Nela is your grandmother, not your mami, see. He explained it all to me slowly, practically drawing it out in the dirt, the littlest of the cousins visiting from the capital, and I thought that kids from Quito were weird and stupid. Fragile, bright-red creatures who eat their own boogers and crap in their pants. Dumb little kids who are always getting itchy and rashy, kids who the sun just destroys, who the ocean batters and spits back out. I never understand why they make me play with them.

When Ñaña Teresa, who lives in Quito, visits with her husband, they both talk strangely inward, like they're whispering to their necks. Their sons are pale, with wide mouths and light eyes, and everybody makes a fuss over them, they practically force me to entertain them. Sometimes they bring their cousins from the capital too, all older than me, but short and stunted like chow chows.

I soon get tired of playing and I go up to the parlor to sit with my ñañas, but they make me go back down. Mija, you're like an old woman, what's the matter with you, go play with the other kids. So I go down again to play with that string of bright-red kids all smelling like clothes forgotten in the bottom of a drawer, but it drives me crazy that they don't know anything. And when I don't understand the words they use, like *la Playstashun, la Play, los Nikes, los stikers, el shopin*, in here under this shed it's *full darc*, they laugh at me. This kid don't know what la Play is?

Don't call me kid, my name is Ainhoa.

And those sonofabitches fall all over themselves laughing. I climb up in my guava tree and I stay there, ignoring them. They shout up at me, come down, Ainhoa, or, come down, negrita. When they call me negrita, I fill with rage. I stand on the branch of the guava tree, pull aside one leg of my shorts, and I piss on them. They run off, but even so, some piss sprinkles down on their heads. Since I know they're going to tell on me, I hurry down to wash my hands and play the fool. The gringa. The one who wouldn't hurt a fly, which is what I know how to do best. I don't like to play with them because they play rough, dirty pig games.

I tell them let's play dancing, or let's go up to my room and read books. I invite them out to the street to play dodgeball or catch, to dress up like Pimpinela or Mari Trini, I tell them I'll be the redheaded woman from the Pimpinela duo and one of them can be the man and we'll sing. Let's rock ourselves in the hammocks until we fall out onto the vinyl floorboards. Let's ask the ñañas to take us to the beach to build mermaids out of sand or make mud pies. But no, they only want to hide under the wooden shed in the backyard, where we keep extra coconuts and tools, to look at each other's coochies and weenies.

 I don't like to do that.

 It makes me feel nausea, rage, and shame.

I go up to the parlor where all the adults are dancing and eating like animals and I tell my ñañas I just want to stay there, but they say, go on down, mija, go on down, mamita, you're getting old before your time, mi amor. Go on and play, go on and be a little girl, mijita. So I go back downstairs, but I don't go under the shed because I don't want anyone to see my punani. Because it's mine.

Before she goes to work, my Mami Checho bathes me and she tells me, mijita, this is your punani, nobody else's.

Nobody can touch it, only me or the ñañas to bathe you. If someone touches your punani, you have to tell me about it.

That's why I tell them, you all are pigs for showing each other your coochies and your weenies. I tell them, you're pigs for touching each other, for putting your fingers in each other, you're disgusting. They run after me, throwing chunks of dirt, but they can't catch me. I'm the tallest, and I know how to climb trees, they only know how to sit around eating each other's boogers.

In one of their many visits for Carnaval, they took us to the beach like always. We divided ourselves up in the cars of the bright-red Quito cousins and in Papi Manuel's truck to go to the Las Palmas beach. Pretty soon the ñañas and the new Quiteño family started to drink, to eat, to shriek with laughter like a bunch of idiots, to grind up on each other. Us kids stuffed ourselves with fried pork and milkshakes, and while I chewed, I thought about Noris's face as we left, sad because she wanted to go to the beach too, but they left her behind to take care of my little sister. I don't understand this way of being a family.

I was so sorry for her that before we left I hesitated, I told my Mami Checho that I wanted to stay behind with Noris and my ñañita. Look, mija, just get down here and don't talk nonsense, she yelled at me from the front porch with the bags all ready and a big straw hat to cover herself, because my mami detests the sun. I ran downstairs like I'd been stuck with spurs, leaving behind the long faces of the two little women who wouldn't get to see the ocean in Carnaval.

After watching the party and swimming for hours, making the monsters from Quito swim like starfish, opening our arms and legs and letting the waves push us, swallowing enough salty water to feel like fish, holding our eyes open under the water until we were crying from the salty sting. Much later after eating two whole plates of fried pork and plantains, two coconut, pineapple, and strawberry milkshakes, and fighting with one of my cousins until he got an ass full of sand, it was night and I was sleepy and my Papi Manuel opened up the truck for me to sleep inside.

   I dreamed that I was asleep up high in the guava tree, clinging to the round fruits as if they were my Mami Checho's breasts, as if I were my little ñañita suckling milk from the worms in the guavas, when suddenly the red boys from the capital burst in, their swimsuits wet and sandy, as if the sun were still out up there in the sky.

   Aren't you all cold? No, this isn't cold, it's hot still. And I thought, these people are from another world.

   Tato lost a game and he has to do a dare, they barked.

   They grabbed me by my hands and legs before I could ask anything. Immobilized me. I tried to call out for my ñañas, for anyone, but the timba beat sounded at high volume from the Las Palmas boardwalk. Even inside the car we could hardly hear each other.

   Tato, with his witchy face and eyes so green they gave me chills, was skinny and quiet, but he was always staring at me in a spooky way, sometimes without blinking, without shifting his gaze, until I would throw dirt at him, or sand or water. Now he climbed up on top of me, clawing his way up my body, and his rigid damp sandiness broke into the warmth I had made in the clothes and dry blankets my Mami Checho had arranged around me.

Outside, the dancers shrieked, the laughter and the son of a foundryman, singing about his dream come true, as Tato kissed me hard and I couldn't move. He stuck his tongue in and moved it from one tooth to another, from my tongue to the roof of my mouth, as if he wanted to sing an alien song through my full lips, delivering a mouth of bones into my involuntary silence, drowning in spit.

I couldn't breathe and Tato kept moving over me, his chest bare and wet, his blue bikini with the word *Speedo* on it shining iridescently in the faint glow that entered through the windows of my papi's whorehouse Ford. He had his weenie between my legs, and then I felt how he pulled open one side of my rainbow-colored bathing suit and rooted around flaccidly near the few hairs that had sprouted there. Their ratlike laughter scurried around my head, and in the background, far away, I could hear the muffled laughter of my ñañas beneath the sound of the ocean and the music, which seemed in that moment an ocean fiercer than the ocean of the Las Palmas beach. The singer demanding love, swearing he'll never let you down. Tato shifted his hands up, gripping me hard so

I couldn't move and I felt fear and an urge to hit, but the boys' hands were like tentacles, like suckers stuck to my skin.

And now you are boyfriend and girlfriend forever. They let go and ran off into the night like a pack of wet beasties. Like a five-headed monster.

6.

Voluntad de Dios

It was an early Saturday morning when my Mami Checho and my Papi Manuel took us to visit the lot where they were going to build the so-called house. The house we needed so much so we could stop living on top of each other like animals, my mami said. I don't understand why we can't keep on being animals. We all got into my Papi Manuel's whorehouse Ford, my Mami Checho, my Ñaña Antonia, my Ñaña Tita, and me. As always, they didn't let Ñaña Rita go, and she watched us leave from the door that looks out onto the passageway with the cistern, screeching in her pink robe.

Since my papi's truck is getting older and stiffer by the day, like a cowskin stretched out in the sun, to get it to start we had to push it, we had to beg God to please let it work, we had to caress it so it would grudgingly agree to move us from one place to another. When the beast finally gave in, we went straight down Calle México, all the way.

Whenever we go down Calle México, we turn left, to Las Palmas, to swim, to eat fried pork and sweet plantain fritters, but this time was different. This time my papi turned right and I felt a surge of deep fear, a terror. I thought we were going over to the bad side. Papi, that's the wrong way, you're confused.

But he wasn't confused. We passed the El Cabezón highway, and with my eyes on the Esmeraldas River and those big islands full of green trees, a green that could blind me, I thought about the new house and the distance that would separate me from Mami Nela's house, my real house. We arrived at the police barracks and we kept going, without turning back to our normal life, without even a stutter, farther than anything we'd ever seen before. We went over the bridges and we saw the fairgrounds full of people buying clothes wholesale, so many people among cotton candy machines, carts selling colored popcorn and cold coconut water, feuding with the calm of the skinny guayacán trees filling the side of the highway.

We arrived at the statue of a lion that I had only seen before on visits to the ranch, or day trips to the countryside. Or when we go back to Limones, the island where all us women were born and from where they fled with us, because they say that out there the girls get pregnant early and better to bring them to the city and watch over them jealously, like a statue of San Antonio.

The highway seemed never-ending and my Papi Manuel just kept on driving. I started to get impatient and angry, where are we going, Papi? But that day everyone acted like I didn't exist, they stuck me there in the middle and didn't even talk to me. I thought about pissing myself, but my Mami Checho had warned me that I was getting too big for that foolishness.

Along the highway it was all trees and desolation; trees, dogs, and cats tattooed on the asphalt by the wheels of some semitruck. Trees growing out of the cement shoulder and trees growing out of the cracks in the houses. Trees and tiny little stands selling fresh sugarcane juice, local food, and salted fish, trees and covered trucks with boys and men up on the roof, trees and more trees and a green dizziness. A blinding green, an impossible maddening green.

It was so desolate that I felt even more fear, more rage, more urge to piss myself, but I didn't do anything.

Growing up is not being able to open your mouth when something bothers you, I thought. I didn't say it out loud; anyway, no one was listening to me.

After a long way, we turned left and went down a track that had been recently paved. We arrived halfway down a wide street that had an enormous tree right in the middle. It seemed like the tree was growing from the asphalt and its branches stretched down to the ground like hair. I was sure that at any moment that tree was going to get up and run away, like the thousand-year-old giant it really was, escape from all the people over the riotous green mountains.

Around the tree were women selling fruit, corviche, and green plantain empanadas, and there, in the middle of the weeds, a wooden fence encircled another bit of dirt. Here it is, said my Mami Checho. And I asked, here's what, here's nothing. Again no one responded. The ñañas, my Mami Checho, and my Papi Manuel walked around the lot saying things that made no sense, as if suddenly they and I spoke two different languages. Soon another truck arrived and a fat man got out to talk and show off more dirt in the middle of the dirt, green in the middle of the green.

And we're supposed to live here in the middle of this bush? I yelled desperately. Silence. I started to feel like I couldn't breathe. I was suffocating for no reason. Everything around me went blurry. The trees started to lose the outline that made them trees, the dirt, dirt, and us, people, and the heads of my ñañas floated like winking fireflies above my head.

I collapsed in a heap because I, too, had lost my outline and I had mixed with all the other things; I was also an earthy-green mass, a blurred expanse. They picked me up out of the dirt and put me in the car. The neighborhood was called Voluntad de Dios and that made me feel even more suffocated. Nothing with God in its name brings anything good. For Godssake! my Papi Chelo would cough out before taking Noris out to the backyard to punish her with his belt; trembling, the ñañerío would turn up the volume on the radio, but I still knew what was happening. Or ¡ay, dios mío! my Mami Nela would cry out before closing herself and the ñañas in her room to pray, muttering for one, two, three, four, five, six hours, and then they would come out all red, suffocating, gulping back their snot and their tears.

Let's pray to God, Mami Nela would say when she woke me up at four in the morning. Even if I didn't have the urge, she would force me to take a shit, and then sit me down to read the Bible. Ñaña Antonia, I don't want to live here. Mija, don't worry, she said, smiling like always. It's a long way off, the house isn't even built yet. You act like a little old lady, mijita, be more like a little girl, don't worry so much, and she started singing me to sleep with a Jeanette song.

7.

An inflatable papi

My Papi Manuel loves music.

He loves music so much that whenever he's home he starts up his record player, connects it to the stereo speakers, and then the music never stops. My Papi Manuel loves music so much that he has two suitcases full of black vinyl records that he only brings out of the bedroom on weekends, spinning songs from morning till late at night.

His music can be heard through all the rooms of my Mami Nela's house, on the porch, in the yard, and by the cistern. The music goes running up and down the walls. After making the rounds, the sounds bury themselves in the backyard among the fruit trees and the herbs that can cure espanto de agua and vaginal drop.

My Papi Manuel loves music, whiskey, and tobacco, all at the same time, like a salsa-powered steam engine, a salsa-powered steam engine that reads and sings in chorus.

My Papi Manuel smells like leather, tobacco, and whiskey, like a steam engine that dances, sings, and reads in chorus, all at the same time.

My Papi Manuel smells like an engine, like his old whorehouse truck, which is the smell of salsa, timba, son cubano, guaguancó, gozadera, rumba, the smell of a laborer. I like to smell that smell on my papi, although sometimes he doesn't want anyone to touch him.

He's like an old car, always puffing smoke and playing music.

I try to be a part of his playing, of his easy way of being in the house.

I help him take off his boots when he gets home from his job at the electric company. I like knowing that the lights in the houses turn on thanks to him and his friends climbing up the lampposts, like winged animals or monkeys trapped in a newly built city, messing with the cables to turn on the glow when the sun drops behind the Guacharaca hill. When he gets home from work, I ask him if he wants to eat, and I pretend to be hungry too, so I can keep him company. I eat to the sound of his molars crushing the rice, beans, and fish, I gorge myself to the sound of his mouth slurping up tapao stew, lentil or beef bone soup, his favorite.

I always like my Papi Manuel to tell me things about the world. I know how it works, this world we live in, but I act like a gringa, an idiot. A shameless floozy, like my Mami Nela shouts at Noris when she spies her talking to boys through the garden fence, on the street, or by the cistern, so that my Papi Manuel will tell me ridiculous things. So my papi will blow the words into my face, with his skunk breath of smoke and chilled whiskey, the smell of a laborer.

So my papi will tell me to be serious, or ask me if I'm crazy.

I say, Papi, why did Papi Chelo leave?

He lowers his newspaper, takes off his glasses, which turn brown when the sun shines in through the parlor windows, fans himself a little with the pages, and unbuttons one of the pearly buttons on his red shirt. He clears his throat and says, mija, your Papi Chelo bone out, you hear? and I ask him what does that mean to bone out, is it because he's good-looking or what, and he just looks at me, his brown eyes behind his brown lenses, no idea what shit is going through my head. No, mija, he just bone out, you hear? Just that, mija, people leave, you hear? It's just how things go, mamita, there's nothing to understand.

And I laugh to myself, but not in his face. I put on

my serious mug because I love these dumb answers my papi gives me.

I know Papi Chelo is screwing another woman out on the ranch. Everybody knows it.

I know because I heard the whispers of it's not the first time and it won't be the last either.

That once he stayed out there six months and didn't even send money for food.

My Mami Nela, like all teachers, is always broke. They always pay her late, she's always having to pawn some piece of gold jewelry to eat. But that time, before I was born, they say, the hunger was so bad in this house that my ñañas and my mami had to take in washing from strangers.

Of course, they couldn't tell Mami Nela, she could have died from the shame, to raise her daughters to be slaves, no, never. But there was no other way to bring in food. Food that my ñañas gave to Ñaña Catucha, so she could pretend that she brought it to the house as a gift. Like it was hers.

And I just keep filling up his cloud of salsa with my questions.

A crazy welter of questions that fills me when my

papi is sitting on the couch, surrounded by his black vinyl records. Square red and orange record sleeves, with pictures of far-off beach sunsets, palm trees framing groups of women in little bikinis. Papery record sleeves with skinny smiling men posing in their fuchsia shirts with hibiscus trees and thick mustaches, with white pimp shoes, blindingly white like the little baggies that my papi sometimes keeps in the glove compartment. Vinyls spilling Cuban voices out through the speakers he connects to his untouchable turntable.

Papi, why don't I have light eyes like you? He lowers his head and laughs, clearing his throat, mijita, be serious. If your eyes were this color, the boys would be after you already, just take it easy.

And I go crazy trying to decode the madness and the many worlds that are born from my papi's mouth, like the fungus growing on the damp trunks fallen on the ground way in the back of the yard. Like the worms in the wounds of the dogs, no explanation, just because.

Sometimes my papi does my hair, but he's terrible at it.

First he scratches at my scalp with the comb till it's raw, and then he gathers this wild forest spirit of hair into two balls that look like the sacks of the black bull out on Papi Chelo's ranch.

I think I look hideous, but I don't say anything,

because I know this papi is doing his best. He's a loony, but he's trying. He does my hair ugly, dresses me all gangster, as my Mami Nela says, and takes me out to the beach. He scoops me up in the whorehouse, which is itself louder than the music he turns on so he won't have to talk to me, and then he makes me jog along the sand from end to end of Las Palmas. I try to keep up with his rhythm; my heart gallops and I follow after him like a street dog running after any old motorcycle. Finally he meets up with a pack of men who all dress like him and talk like him. Men in flowered shirts with colorful buttons whose eyes are always reddened, really red, as if they had gone into the ocean with them open.

They go away behind the palm trees, and I play the fool and mess around in the sand as smoke billows behind those trees, but not a normal smoke, a thick smoke like out in the countryside when they're burning a sick cow that's no good for eating. And then my papi comes out from behind those trees a cheerful sonofabitch, happy as if he'd seen God. Or maybe the Devil—which for him, born in Montalvo, would be the same as seeing God.

My Papi Manuel tells me all about his adventures with fantastical creatures. Even though my Mami Checho doesn't like it, I always ask him in front of her: Papi, tell me about the time you fought the goblin, and my mami, angry, for what you wanna tell those lies to the girl, Manuel. Mijita, don't repeat that nonsense your papi tells you, ok? Goblins don't exist! my Mami Checho yells, as she leaves early in the morning in her secretary clothes.

When she's not around, he not only tells me about goblins but also about the millionaires who made a pact with the Devil, and their hacienda out near his father's ranch, my grandfather who I've never met. I call him grandfather and not papi because my mami says he's an alcoholic and that she'll never take me to meet him. Out in Montalvo, the Tello family ranch had a caretaker who was an old monkey, and instead of a nutsack he had a bunch of keys hanging down under his weenie. And their bulls were huge, ay mijita, those beasts were gigantic, you hear? But you never saw more than three cows, even though they supplied the meat for the whole town, always the same three dumb open-mouthed cows. Serious business, mijita.

Sometimes my Papi Manuel takes me to do things I don't understand. But I know it's just cuz he's a loony. He drives out to Isla Piedá and we wait for hours, and finally two big Black men appear, really big and black, wearing long baggy T-shirts and combs on their heads, with gold chains and gold teeth and gold braids and they give him little baggies that he hides in the glove compartment like little earthy-green treasures. Ainhoa, mija, little girls don't go around talking about grown-up business, you hear? And I look back at him and smile with my idiotic gringa face and I tell him I want a hamburger and some fried pork, and he laughs as he steers the beast to my favorite food truck.

My papi can't say no to me.

I know that all I have to do is stare hard and push a little for him to give way, to cough up anything I want from him. Because a little girl always wants more from her papi, always. A papi is like a stick of gum that you chew without stopping, desperately, until the flavor is all gone, forever.

Once I dreamed that I had a huge dog with Papi Manuel's face, with his same mug.

A black dog that, instead of barking, drooled out noises that smelled of whiskey and songs by Ray Barretto and Héctor Lavoe. A "Préstame tu mujer," hermano, with a background of "Qué lío," ayúdame, dios, I want to forget, I love her too much. In the dream, which at times is also a nightmare, as the smell of whiskey pours into my guts, enters through my ass to nest in the depths of my belly forever, I call to him, Papi, tssss! tssss! Come along to the beach with me. And the dog at first acts the lazy, but finally he has no choice but to follow me.

To me, that's my Papi Manuel. A dog that doesn't bark, that instead of howling, sings salsa music, the mouth of an incurable, shaggy partier, the bozal of a mulatto god, just like him.

A dog pretending, in the nightmare, that he doesn't want to eat his own shit, but he does it anyway, an obedient and lying animal, an inflatable papi.

A no señor,

no man,

no husband,

no papi.

A beautiful inflatable clown, of whiskey and sea glass, landed by accident in the world of fathers.

8.

Mami Checho is water

Water that won't stay still, unsteady water, like in an earthquake when you're by chance looking straight at a tank brimful with water. Your vibrating face trapped in that liquid mirror as your reflection slowly loses its shape, loses its focus, abandons the shape of a little girl's face, and starts to look more like an amoeba or the drawing of a cell in an illustrated science page you can buy at the five-and-dime for a few sucres.

A trembling, strange water in the middle of a volcano. Like the volcano that everyone says is buried under the Las Palmas beach, a giant ear canal that someday will swallow us all up and turn us into legend, like the tales my Papi Manuel starts spinning that nobody believes, because as you listen you can't make any little pictures form inside your head. When the ear canal of the volcano expels its water, people will say, Esmeraldas? What's that? And they will be drawn by the stories of a race passed beyond life, hidden from the salt water, and there they will find the fragments of our existence. But no one will be able to truly know what we were.

When I start talking like that, out loud to myself, my Mami Checho stares at me with a face surprised and worried. As if she were saying to me with her worried squint, ay, missy, talking nonsense again, mamita, mijita, why do you say such strange things. Mamita, come back down to earth. That's what she always tells me, keep your feet on the ground, mamita, there's a reason us humans can't fly. And I ask her about airplanes, Mami, airplanes make it so that humans can fly. And she laughs, ay, yuyi, missy, you got an answer for everything, when you grow up you should study to be a lawyer, you hear? You must have that pointy tongue for something, missy, because that tongue of yours is serious business. In my time they'd have bust your lip already for talking back to the grown-ups. I let you go on, mijita, but only as long as you keep those long-ass feet on the ground, those dancing legs good and set on the ground, mamita, and leave off inventing all that damned nonsense. Just try to be a little girl, a normal little girl.

Without a doubt my Mami Checho is a woman of water. I can see the waves through her beautiful skin; through her flirty smile I can see the unending water of my mami swelling, becoming mist.

That's it, my Mami Checho mists, sprinkling her charm like water over everything. With her secretary's skirt and her nylon stockings she's like a water tank treated with insecticide, nothing dull about her. Water is hard to grasp, mysterious. No matter how clear and calm it looks, it can still be the perfect home for a bunch of shit that will mess you up.

The water tanks breed mosquitoes, or the swampy puddle begins to turn green, and if you drink it, you'll have the runs for ten days straight. I know because I've drunk from all the liquids stagnating in my Mami Nela's garden, I've even drunk the water that's born from my coochie, and I would love to drink my mami like when I was a baby and I nursed from her. But those are things I can't say out loud because she gets all spooked.

The first time I drew my mami, I made the curvy outline of her body with large breasts and wide hips, and

I colored in her skin blue on top of green, which is the color of the water on the island we come from. The art teacher told me, humans don't have that skin color, angel baby, use a different one. But I told her, miss, you haven't seen my mami up close. She just laughed. To grown-up people everything we say from our small bodies is a joke. But no, my Mami Checho is water and the color of her skin has the funny greenish tone of the sea of Limones.

But water is like that, traitorous and lying like my Mami Checho. You can never really come to understand the water. I know that my Mami Checho started out cleaning the library where now she's a secretary; I also know that she's very smart, even though as a little girl she was the dumbest in the house, the one with no future, the sickly little girl that nobody wanted around. And that somehow her desire to be fierce and mysterious has to do with that old past as thick, dumb, empty-headed.

My Mami Checho was born sickly, ugly, and undernourished, with a murmur in her heart, which I understand like a little wind that doesn't connect to what it should connect to inside her body.

My Mami Nela worked as a rural schoolteacher, in one of those schools so far away that to get there you have to get up at three in the morning, go by covered truck, canoe, and horse, to give classes to kids who are really grown-ups who still don't know how to read or write or add or subtract; Mami Nela taught all that and more. She taught them a little of everything, and she counseled the girls to not get pregnant, to study a lot, and to make it to the city. Since she was so busy and she didn't know what to do with this weak, sickly little girl that she had birthed, my Mama Doma stepped in.

Mama Doma tried all her cures on her little Chechito. She brushed her with goatweed, made her kalanchoe tea, bathed her with achiote leaves, gave her noni and bitter nightshade. She took her to the only doctor she trusted, Doctor Minda. Whenever a pregnant woman didn't have enough money to pay, Doctor Minda would tell her, look, amiga, go in good faith to Doña Doma, she can help you with your child, tell her I sent you and that I send my compliments. But even that doctor said, Domita, there's no cure for this baby, she needs an operation and for that we have to take her all the way to Quito and it costs money. Mama Doma left with her swaddled little girl but no idea what to do. She went back to her house on Eloy Alfaro, stuffed a change of clothes into a bag, and said to everyone, I'll be back.

The whole family was shocked, hey, mamita, where are you going? Wait, come back. I'm taking one last chance to save my little girl. So Mama Doma walked to the Costeñita bus station in Calle Malecón, caught a covered truck to La Tola, the last tip of land at the north of Esmeraldas, boarded a motorboat, and went on to Limones. It was the end of October and the islands were already curing the balsa wood, decorating the Black saints, tuning the drumheads, and harvesting the seeds to fill the guasá rattles for the celebration of San Martín de Porres.

At the dock, two fishermen recognized her and helped her off the boat. Mama Doma sat anxiously on a wooden bench, as people and baggage from all over continued to disembark, coming to celebrate their saint. There she sat, looking out over the green sea, the flying roots of the mangroves, and the manta rays jumping, saluting her journey.

Next to the dock was the wooden niche with the small Black saint, decorated with lace and colored ribbons, with his straw hat, his brown cassock, and his blackity-black skin. Mama Doma approached gently, raising up her swaddled Chechito, and said to San Martín, I deliver to you this little girl, Saint, from now onward let it be according to your will and to God's.

The story always ends there, and I say, But, Mami Checho, what then? What did Mama Doma do then? How did she come back, what did she eat on the trip, mamita, I want to know more. And she, ay, yuyito, the important thing is that I am alive thanks to the saint,

I still have the murmur but I'm full of life, mamita. So alive that I could bring to this earth my two princesses, you and your sister. But I want to know more, I always want to know more about the stories and about everything. Since she won't tell me all of it, my only option is to invent the stories myself, to complete them in a feverish craze high up in the guava tree:

Mama Doma cried as she waited for the saint to fulfil the miracle, when suddenly the arrullo singers and the bombo drummers burst out of their houses, drumming their cununos and shouting their songs:

> San Martín has arrived
> in Limones
> he brought doves
> cooing lullabies
> he brought doves
> arrulladoras.

The voices and the bodies in hats and turbans printed in brown and orange, sweaty from shouting and drinking whiskey, wrapped around Mama Doma. They made a sweet circle with her in the middle, without ever stopping their song:

> San Martín has arrived
> in Limones
> he brought doves
> arrulladoras.

Mama Doma waited for a sign of life, and then the little girl cried out. Nothing like the cry of a baby to know that it's healthy. So she followed the singers and the crowd and went dancing up onto the barge, along with the priest and the dancers. That enormous floating metal platform, which seems too big to be moved at all, but it's pulled by one little motorboat, covered with flowers and fruits, leaves from the coconut palm and marimbas beating desperately, as if they weren't celebrating the saint at all but the coming of the end of the world.

On the barge, the arrullo singers continue their chorus to the Black saint until they arrive in Canchimalero, another nearby island. While the barge and the other fishing boats with their saints and their drums slowly come in to dock on the coast of Canchimalero, all the little girls and boys on the beach, wet with salt water, reach out their hands to receive fruits and gifts from the voyagers, as they say that San Martín himself gave, in his own small boat, with a little basket from which the fruits, fish, and bread never ceased to flow.

Then Mama Doma got down with her little Chechito, swaddled up in that way so her legs would grow straight, and she joined the procession of bodies carrying Black saints of all different sizes. She grabbed a red string, knowing that if she took a string she would have to return next year to the Festival of San Martín and not take any string—because the Black saint is a jealous saint, they say. He gives, but he also takes away.

So Mama Doma danced and drank whiskey, cradling her little girl, among shots fired into the air from hands loaded with gold rings, in the fumes of the herbal grain alcohol brought in the boats from Borbón. When the mass began with the white bishop dressed up in African robes, Mama Doma went over to the food stalls and ate up a plate of guanta in coconut sauce. Then she got into another boat, with a boy who recognized her for helping his mama give birth, and he took her from Canchimalero to Borbón. In Borbón she was recognized too, walking to catch the truck back to Esmeraldas, and before they let her go they loaded her down with bags of coconuts, a bunch of salted fish, one of smoked ray, two cheeses wrapped in palm leaves, and more bags of milk.

All this I imagine up among the branches; I tell it to the fruits and the worms, and also to the leaves. Above all, to the leaves, because their greenery makes me think about the living water that is my Mami Checho.

My mami has as many secrets as the water. I know she is alive because I see how life springs up around her, how people's voices turn toward her, how the water that comes from within her made possible my existence and my ñaña's. But I'm not sure if all that giving of life makes her really alive. I don't know if all that giving love makes her really love herself.

I always have the feeling that she's about to get up and run out and leave us all behind. Although usually she denies it, I see her looking restless on the weekends, sick of laying up in the parlor or her bedroom, which has been hers since Mama Doma passed away, when Mami Checho was seventeen, and which she has shared with my Papi Manuel since they got married, when she was eighteen.

My Mami Checho always talks about her life with Mama Doma as a kind of happy dream. She was glad to have been saved by her grandmother, to have learned to heal, and to have been adored by a woman as sweet as Doma Cuero. Whenever my Mami Checho came back to visit her parents' house, this house where all us women live, she always felt uncomfortable because they made her clean and cook. Things that she didn't know how to do, because her grandmother protected her and sheltered her, maybe too much. My Mami Checho tells me about the people, the many hundreds of people who went to Mama Doma to be healed. That even an English nun took lessons from her. Mama Doma never charged her, but the nun would bring pretty clothes for Mami Checho, and so the whole neighborhood thought that she was a gringa too, because her hair was so long and because, unlike other girls, they never saw her put one foot out in the street.

She really never stepped out in the street because Mama Doma protected her so that nobody could go and make her good little girl pregnant. But one Carnaval, by chance they sent her out to buy a Coke with Irene, the girl who looked after her, and Chechito's legs took her right off the rails. A bucketful that slips out of your hands and immediately becomes mud with the dry earth of the yard. Like water my mami ran to Las Palmas, because a liquid always wants to escape through any little crack, like sometimes when I laugh so hard a little pee escapes, which is a kind of water that has to come out so my body doesn't explode.

Scared, Irene said to Chechito, let's go back, or they'll punish us. But Irene didn't know that my mami wasn't any longer the seventeen-year-old girl who wasn't allowed to even walk down the block, but a wild, teeming water, like the water in the pools where they farm shrimp. Dip your foot in there and you could go right through to China, like digging through the sand to escape to a world of strange tongues and different bodies.

Anyway, there they were, in the middle of the Las Palmas boardwalk, with no permission from nobody; Chechito and Irene stood there uncovering the meat of a city that they didn't really know. A place full of bums in rainbow-colored clothes and untidy Afros; a beach town where everyone partied till dawn, but these girls went to bed at nine at night. These girls who only saw the dawn in a vigil at the bedside of a laboring woman or a wounded patient, who knew nothing about endless parties, nothing about the delicious tangle of bodies. That life was denied them.

When Chechito tells me about this, her only secret escape, this disobedience born from her navel, like everything that is born in Carnaval, I realize that without Carnaval I might never have been born.

When she talks about that funny moment, when she met my Papi Manuel by accident, and how she was embarrassed when he invited her to dance because he spoke to her in English. Since he'd never seen her before, he thought she was a gringa, and then he was sure of it because Chechito couldn't even two-step.

I watch the water rise up in her chest, under her breastbone with its blanket of skin, her chest covered with delicious breasts that smell heavenly, the scent of calm and comfort. That same chest fills with a slime, like an oozing snail, that water they squirt from their one and only foot that looks like an enormous damp coochie and leaves a ripple of mucus smelling of shellfish in its wake.

To be alive thanks to the novelty of Carnaval makes me crazy. I like to be alive knowing that my Mami Checho left her house for just a few hours, swept along by the velocity of the water boiling in her coochie. I feel that boiling too, when December ends and everybody starts throwing water at each other right on New Year's Day. But the truth is, if you were to ask me what my Mami Checho is like, if a quiz at school said, describe what your mother looks like, I wouldn't be able to write anything normal. Because my Mami Checho isn't normal, she's like pooled water once it's released, breathing out a beautifully greenish-brown reek, loosing animals ready to burrow into the earth and parasites that we can't see with our eyes or our tongue.

My Mamita Checho has the beauty of a pond, an invisible beauty that comes alive when she gets angry and sings badly the lyrics to the songs that she doesn't understand and doesn't like. She's a still water that doesn't know how to dance, that seems to have been placed here by an alien creature, forced to live in this house, with this ñañerío. The same alien that brought her to Las Palmas and said to her, that skinny Black guy with eyes the color of honey is going to be the father of your children and your husband. Although you share nothing but a mutual desire, he will be your husband. Although you are a sheltered little girl and he is a communist laborer bum and a drunk, that will be your husband, carajo, and that's all there is to it. But still I go through the ritual of telling the leaves of the guava tree what my Mami Checho is like. I shimmy up with my long, flat, dancing feet on the branch of the tree, I cling to the branches with an unbelievable ease, as if this were the place I truly belong, and not the earth that my mami tells me again and again to keep my feet on. To learn that I belong there and not to the height of the trees, which is where I feel happy. Up high in the trees where nobody can tell me what to do or make me talk about things I don't understand.

The trees, especially the guavas, understand my language, even though it never communicates anything directly. If I tell them that my Mami Checho is a pond that smells deliciously rotten, but looks beautiful as anything, and that the only way I can find calm in the tumult of confusion always going on in this neighborhood is by smelling her chestnut-colored skin with its open pores, the guava tree sways, dapples the green of its leaves in my face, and shows me that mamis, in their silence and their exile from this territory, can also love. I don't get to see my Mami Checho very much, and when I have her close to me I stuff myself between her big breasts to take in the smell of the milk that means she's alive, but she gently pulls me away and says, go bathe, mamita, go get rid of that pig smell that's stuck to you from being up there in the trees, sunning yourself like a poor soldier. And I go running off to bathe and scent myself with my Little Women perfume and then I look for my mami again to stuff myself now clean, now human like her, into her chest, but my clean and human mami has gone flying away, gushing into the earth, or she's already trickled through the cracks of the wood floor, she's dried up in the sun or she's turned into a puddle where the invisible animals hide away, and life makes more life beyond what the eye can see.

My Mami Checho is water and water can't be held in your two hands, never. No matter how much you like its color, and the reflection of your kinky head in it, we can't catch water in our hands, we can only catch it with our snout. That's why I drink my mami. When she's not looking, I glug-glug, glug-glug and she doesn't even notice, but in my head I am taking from her life to live my life, I'm like those parasites that grow in the water, silent, invisible, dirty, not-human, that take life and live beyond the water. I know that when my mami isn't here anymore, I will still be here and I will have surpassed her cannibalized water, I will have been, finally, the life beyond her life.

The subterranean water that we can never see.

9.

Chamber pot

Esta rabadilla que no me da
que la tengo tiesa como un compás
manteca de iguana le voy a untar
para que se mueva pa'lla y pa'ca

This little rump of mine, it just won't work
got it stiff and stuck like a rusty clock
with iguana grease I'm gon' butter it up
get it to move all round the block

My Mami Nela sings to me with a crooked rhythm, like her crooked tooth. The blackest of all us women, blackity-black and huge like an ancient tree, the tree that holds up our house. My Mami Nela is from the north, from the island of Limones. Tall and solid, she has the largest breasts I've ever seen in my life, two avocados overfull and ripened by the sun.

Perched on her bed, I watch her dry her enormous breasts after her morning bath, applying lotions, creams, and powders to the folds of those two heavy bodies. Then with theatrical movements she fastens on her black Peter Pan brassiere, the only one with the capacity to lift such voluptuousness. Breasts that fed all my ñañas, that could easily feed an entire battalion, the whole neighborhood, or even the whole city.

The largest share of her morning toilet consists in drying her breasts and powdering them to avoid strong odors from the sweat produced by the navy-blue slacks and white shirt with black pearly buttons of her teacher's uniform. She also combs her hair, softened with straightener and tinted with Bigen dye, into a small ponytail. Sometimes, when it's not so hot and there's a breeze flowing from the sea, she puts brown powder on her cheeks and a little mascara, but what she never, ever forgets is the wine-red lipstick outlining her delicate mouth.

Like almost everyone who's born in Limones, when Mami Nela was still a little girl Mama Doma brought her to the city, where she finished primary school and studied in a normal school to become a teacher. More than a vocation, it was one of the few opportunities for women who came from the north: either become a teacher or find a policeman or military man as a husband. Luckily my Mami Nela had a knack for teaching, for forming her students into young people who could do sums, read and recite, cut and glue to perfection.

My Mami Nela, like Mama Doma, is a midwife, healer, half witch. Of course, I could never say to her face that she is a witch, because to say witch is to say the Devil, and she is a fervent Christian, fanatically married to Christ-Our-Savior and the Virgin-Mary-Amen.

My Mami Nela has always had a special sweetness for me. A strange love she gives with a freezing stare, with making me do things I don't want to do, pressing the cold iron to my nipples so my breasts won't sprout, smoothing out my body so I don't grow crooked, molding my face to make it more delicate. From her I learned that that's love, to make others do what they don't want to do, always by the force of your gaze, a smack, or a word. Love is an enema in your ass when you have amoebas swimming around inside you.

My Mami Nela wakes me at four in the morning to shit, and when I was little I had to do it in her own chamber pot, at that hour as cold as the mouth of a corpse. Drowsily, through the veil of the dim light and my sleepiness, that chamber pot seemed enormous.

Like a pool full of the piss of all the ñañas and mamis Nela Loma had woken at four in the morning to piss and shit there, through all her years of child-rearing.

I imagined myself swimming in the fluids of my ñañas and my Mami Checho like a rebirth. After all, somehow the tiny little hole where you piss from connects to the other untouchable hole my Ñaña Antonia told me babies come out of. Or I imagined them all tiny like slugs, or like slugs suddenly growing the faces of my ñañas, swimming around in my piss. All of us mothers and daughters of that old chamber pot in which we've been compelled to piss and shit before the light of day.

She and my Mami Checho together taught me to write, but I really got good at it because my Mami Nela has taken me to the school where she teaches arts and crafts class starting when I was three years old.

Our routine from Monday to Friday was the following: First she made me take a shit, although really sometimes I didn't have anything to offer her. Still, she would sit me on the chamber pot while the radio belted out sorrowful pasillos and boleros, as I pleaded with my flat little ass to offer up something to this lady so she would leave me in peace already. Rarely could I shit in the presence of my Mami Nela, shitting with an audience made me close up completely.

I would say, Mami Nela, please, I don't have the

urge, or it's that I'm sleepy still. With a dry look, grumbling about my rudeness, she would take the chamber pot away.

Then we would sit at the foot of her bed to pray and read the Bible.

My Papi Manuel didn't like it when they made me pray or read the Bible. He said they would aluminate me, or alienate me, or I don't know what nonsense. I just wanted to nod off for good, right there, mouth open. Then she would make me shower in cold water, to wake up the brain, another torture for my cold-blooded body. My bones clacked together, my teeth chattered; I felt like shooting like a snake into some deep hole dug in the earth.

I came out of the bath unable to speak, my teeth eating themselves up in the attempt to re-create some heat.

Then the combing... the dressing.

All so hard and painful, as if my body couldn't feel at all, like she was combing a mango tree that can't tremble when its leaves are plucked; or that trembles without anyone hearing. Since my Mami Nela started doing my hair, pulling chunks out of my scalp like hell, I've stopped plucking leaves off the trees. Even though I would say, Mamita Nela, it hurts, ayayay, please, you're hurting me, she would just keep combing roughly as if she couldn't hear me. Perhaps the pain of the trees is like that, a scream that comes out as a tiny sound my little girl's ear can't decipher. I've always wondered if the trees can feel the pain of the things that happen around them.

I did try to say, Mamita Nela, my head hurts, but she just kept combing and pulling out hair like a sonofabitch. I would see bits of my hair scattered on the clean wood floor, clean enough to eat soup off of, and I would feel like crying.

While Mami Nela went to bathe and get ready and Noris served breakfast, I would gather up all the bits of my hair in my two hands and secretly bury them between my two trees: the guava tree and the chirimoya tree.

Finally, we would eat a big breakfast to have enough energy to walk all the way to school.

Whenever I sleep in my Mami Nela's bed, I have vivid, oppressive dreams; nightmares and terrors that lead nowhere.

Some time ago I dreamed that the hairs I had buried between the trees in the backyard started to grow roots, to sprout monstrously. From the hair-earth branches grew lumpy balls of fishbait that soon began to show my face, my gestures. In the dream I heard a noise and I came closer until I could really make out those faces, the same as mine, the same fat mouth, the same pointy little witch nose and big horse eyes, all freakishly like mine. When one of the fishbaits told me to stay and chat, I screamed, and there was my Mami Nela, like always, opening the mosquito net to get the chamber pot in which I would have to leave something for her, offer up some piece of rotten insides. Some meaty farts; myself turned to shit so she would leave me in peace.

It was hard for me to understand why I had to sleep with my Mami Nela and not in my room anymore; it was a decision they made all the women together, behind closed doors, without telling me what was going on. It's true that my Papi Chelo once came to my room in the night and got into my bed by mistake.

It's also true that sometimes Noris comes in and I braid her hair.

My Mami Nela told me that I can't go around putting my hands on just anyone, but to me Noris isn't just anyone, she's my ñaña. As much my ñaña as my Ñaña Tita, my Ñaña Antonia, my Ñaña Rita, my Ñaña Catucha. As much my mami as my Mami Checho. She makes me food, she dressed me when I was little, sometimes she takes me to the playground to play, she takes care of my little sister. So why can't I braid her hair?

My Mami Nela doesn't at all like the questions I ask.

I said, Mami Nela, if Noris cooks for me, washes my clothes, sings me songs, and plays with me, why can't I braid her hair? She stared at me, opening real wide the pips of her eyes like the frogs who come into the house out at the ranch when it rains, and I opened my eyes real wide too, and we stayed staring at each other like that for a long time without blinking.

The first time we had a staring contest like that I dreamed that hours passed and years, and neither of us would close our eyes. We both started to cry, but still neither of us would look away.

Each of us just as stubborn as the other, the house began to flood with the salty water from our eyes.

Soon a beach formed and became famous, and like always, rich stinky tourists from the capital came to piss themselves, to puke all over the beach, and to mess with the girls making little houses up in the guava, mango, and chirimoya trees. Given that the house was underwater and a sea of tears forming between mami and daughter, those same little girls had no other option than to open a stand selling fish corviche and deep-fried sweet plantains and to let the tourists screw them, the same tourists vomiting all over the sea of our tears.

Still we didn't look away, and that watery-eyed sea just kept growing, drowning us completely.

The walks to school with Mami Nela made me forget all about the pain in my ass, the impossibility of shitting, the hair pulling, the Bible, and the cold water. Nela Loma turned into the sweetest lady, singing as we walked up and down the hills. Into a grown-up girl, singing with a crooked rhythm and telling stories about my birth, every day the same like a repetitive prayer. Like the repetitive prayers and songs at a wake that make you so heartsick you cry, even if you never met the dead person.

Mija, I only ever drank once in my life; when you were born, I got drunk. I drank to the song of the day, a long ayyyyy from "El llorón," a little girl just broke my heart. How I rejoiced in your birth, mija, my first grandchild. Mi reina, mi niña, my little woman.

And all I could think about was the impossibility of getting to see my Mami Nela party like on the day of my birth.

I thought about how convenient it would be to be born again. To be born every day, over and over.

To come out of my Mami Checho's vagina, one fifth of September like Vico C's daughter, at eleven forty at night, again and again. My round head would appear, stretching my mami's hip bones, tearing a little the meeting point between her coochie and her anus to make my life possible, and then, my Mami Nela's drunkenness.

My Mami Nela who never dances, not even as a joke.

My Mami Nela who's always angry with someone, above all with the ñañerío and the cleaning girls, but never with the ñaños and the boys who carry the sacks of fruits from the ranch.

My Mami Nela, always smiling for the men and bad-mouthing the women. My Mami Nela, always after the ñañas, squashing any sign of heat, that is to say, the normal course of life.

The walk would become long and festive as Nela was hailed by both men and women with respect and affection. Many had been her students, others had been born thanks to her assistance, still others she had cured of espanto, evil eye, fever, malaria, rashes, or itchy skin. Some kids she had saved from growing up with six fingers on one hand, by tying a thread real tight around the extra finger when they had barely come out of their mamis. For some women she had predicted whether their child would be a boy or girl just by staring at their rounded bellies for a few minutes or fondling the swelling of their stomachs; she would say, this belly is a girl, or this one is a boy.

Old women would shout, Nela, mija, God bless you and keep you and your girls, Domita is watching over you from heaven. Others asked her what they could take to wake up early, to improve their memory, to study. In a sweet little girl's voice she would reply, for my girls, I put paico behind their ears, or I put chickweed in their pillowcases. I make them green juices with alfalfa, I make them eliminate before they bathe in the morning. Just look at my little girl here, she learned to read and write practically all by herself! she would say proudly, pointing at me.

But in reality, Nela Loma of the big family house is a police inspector general, a fierce overseer. Is bad-tempered, angry at everyone, except at me. She only gives me that look when I get fidgety, and with that look alone I understand that I need to calm myself down, carajo, leave off my fool jumping around and sit down quietly to read the books my papi and mami give me, sit right down and eat this mashed avocado with sugar, at five in the afternoon, without saying another word.

No matter how much time passes, no matter how hungry we've been at home, the women he's been screwing or the blows he hands out to daughters, men, and cleaning girls all with the same force, when Papi Chelo returns, he's always treated well by my Mami Nela.

No matter if months have passed with only my ñañas and herself bringing food into this house, no matter if women have come by to say, Doña Nela, your husband is out there on the ranch with a younger woman, a little hustler who steals his money. When Papi Chelo returns, she still makes three kinds of seafood encocado, three kinds of juice, three kinds of rice, and salads and fried plantains and different soups.

She kills two or three or four chickens, buys a pig at the butcher's on credit, puts all the girls in line, the ñañas in line, the world in line, God and the Devil in line: to grate coconut meat, fry plantains, chop vegetables, make unending pitchers of juice. To squeeze limes, cut chillangua leaves, sprinkle wild basil, boil huge pots of mint leaves, steep coffee with cinnamon sticks: all to receive Don Chelo.

We all sit down at the long wooden table, Papi Chelo at the head. Sometimes I sit in that chair on purpose, just to test that nobody else can use it, and they yank me right out. The women sit down all around the table in silence, a rare silence that I only feel when Papi Chelo returns to the house. As if everyone in the neighborhood all came to an agreement to calm right down, to lower the volume on the radio speakers, to stop yelling and shouting nonsense; even the wind blows more gently than it should when Papi Chelo's toucan beak is present at our table. Everything happens in silence, everybody's lost their tongue, it's the tongue that we are eating for lunch as my Mami Nela and Noris bring in the plates of food.

Half a table full of plates and juices for Papi Chelo and one medium plate for all the women. No one can get up from the table before Don Chelo, no one but him can talk while we all eat.

After those lunches or dinners, strange things happen. Stifled sobs. Insomnia. Almost none of the ñañas sleep when Papi Chelo returns. Even I wander in my mind without being able to really sleep and I can't find a reason why. Nor do I understand why my Papi Chelo's presence is necessary in this house. The ñañas do everything, the girls and Noris do whatever's left, and my Mami Nela too; and that's without even counting my Mami Checho. For me, papis are things that you can't even really say decorate the house; they mess it up. Above all, Papi Chelo messes up all the women of the house with his mere presence.

One night, before it was decided that I should sleep with Mami Nela, when Papi Chelo returned, he came into my room. I didn't know it was him until I saw his body move toward the window.

I stayed still, watching to see what he would do. He moved clumsily from the window toward my bed, and by instinct I ran to the opposite end from where his body stood. I could hardly see anything, but my room began to fill with the smell of his bitter sweat and his alcoholic breath. It was him, it had to be him. He moved slowly back to the window of my room, which looks out onto the yard, from where you can see my trees: the guava, the chirimoya, and the mango, and in the little triangle of light coming in I could see that he held a gun in his hands. A gun that could have been something else, that I wished was something else, but it was a gun. I know that on the ranches people have them to protect themselves, above all if your ranch is on an island with your last name, surrounded by thickets of mangroves with their aerial roots. You might have to defend yourself from thieves and pirates. But I had never seen a gun in this house, and the color of rusty metal that I glimpsed in the triangle of light from the yard, that's how fear looks: an old drunk holding a rusty gun, and two little eyes searching without knowing where to run. An old drunk defathers himself, turning into a shadow, making you shake uncontrollably.

I heard the muffled shot and a high-pitched cry

that burst in and drowned among my sheets. An inhuman cry that made my bladder explode.

As I drowned in my sheets, more bodies entered the room shouting words that I couldn't make out, reaching out and striking blows all around, while I kept on pissing all over the mattress and the Simpsons coverlet that my Papi Manuel had brought me back from a trip.

The bodies, in a turmoil of cries, took Don Chelo out of my room. I stayed there, frozen.

There was a rare silence in the house, that blind hush settled in my bones for the rest of my life. My Mami Nela came in, she lifted me in her thick black arms and took me to her room. She washed my damp and trembling coochie, she told me, Ainhoa, open your mouth, and she gave me a spoonful of dark liquid that tasted like shit.

I fell into the deepest slumber I've ever felt in this body.

The next day nobody left the house. Noris and the ñañas served breakfast in silence. A vibrating silence that you don't hear with your ears, but you feel in all your bones, and that no one wants to break.

The ñañerío were all wearing dark glasses, my Mami

Checho also with a pair of dark glasses that I had never seen before. My Papi Manuel read the newspaper in the parlor, with his back to us, smoking.

Nobody said a word. I decided that for the first time, I didn't have any questions to ask, and I felt a rage: the sharp rage of not knowing.

I hadn't even finished eating when my Mami Nela came to give me another spoonful of that liquid, that ass liquid of the Devil's herbs, a recipe I never learned. I drank it without saying anything, and then she took me by the hand, as I walked dizzily down the hall to her bedroom.

I couldn't hold it in: Mamita Nela, what's happening to me?

You're growing up, yuyito, that's all that's happening, mija. She arranged the mosquito net, turned off the lamp, and shut the door as I fell unconscious.

10.

Little dugout canoe

My room is an island in the center of my Mami Nela's house, like the little cabin on a boat where any minute a head might pop out, or a narrow compartment inside a barge: a hideout, a cubbyhole built in the parlor with plywood. Wood thin as paper that allows me to hear everything that happens in the parlor or in my Mami Checho and my Papi Manuel's room. Sometimes I hear things that get on my nerves, and then I start singing out loud or I turn on the tape deck and replay songs like crazy, singing over them to distract me from what's going on.

I think it's important sometimes to not know what's happening out there. Like when mosquitoes come buzzing around and you smack at them or shoo them away with palo santo smoke, that's what the voices of people coming in to interrupt me are like, an inconvenient buzzing. But they're easy to turn off.

Through the window I can see my trees: guava, mango, and chirimoya, and sometimes the sky is so blue or so white that I feel like I'm making the crossing in a fishing boat over to Tolita de los Ruano. I'm a fisherman up in my boat, watching a cascade of bass in the dawn, or I'm the Riviel spirit, floating through the dark mangroves in a dugout canoe, scaring all the couples out late at night.

In my room I have a dresser, pink and duck yellow, with eight drawers. In the first drawer I keep my white underpants and my white school uniform shirts. In the second drawer are my underpants with Mickey Mouse, Godzilla, or unrecognizable animals grinning up at me, strange words like *f-a-b-u-l-u-s* in gold glitter and iridescent rhinestones. I adore them but my Papi Manuel says they're spelled badly.

In the third drawer are my dresses and shorts for playing in the garden, the ones I can crawl around in without worrying about tears. In the fourth drawer are my Rugrats T-shirts; once I saw them on TV, but my Papi Manuel explained, mija, the TV makes you alienated, and after that I couldn't stop imagining a silvery full moon growing out of this nose I've inherited from Papi Chelo and I got the shakes and turned it off forever.

In the fifth drawer are my day skirts and dresses, the ones I can't wear to play in the garden, but I can wear to sit in the parlor or go out to the sidewalk or walk to the park with the ñañerío. In the sixth drawer are my bikinis, my one-pieces in all the colors of the rainbow, my swim shorts, and also the teeny thongs that my Mami Checho doesn't let me wear except with a sarong over top, little plastic-covered flowered blouses for swimming at the beach, the pool, and the river. In the seventh drawer, my dresses for parties and holidays, the ones they put me in for a baptism, a kids' party, or a wake-burial. Or to go to mass on Sundays, when Papi Manuel isn't home in the morning and Mami Nela snatches the chance to take me to pray to the saints in the neighborhood church and kiss the little glow-in-the-dark seeds of her rosary.

In the eighth drawer are my books and my journals, the little pink notebooks my Mami Checho gives me so I can write down what doesn't want to come out of my mouth. It's as if an animal were living in my throat, reminding me of the emptiness, of being unable to name the things mutely sleeping in the body. At the same time, it scares my mami when I talk so much out loud, as if I were a politician speechifying or giving mass. I don't know what speechifying is, but I guess the politicians stand up on big platforms, like the Carnaval dancers, and shout strange words into people's faces. My mami feels like that's what I do, like a mini politician. But I don't know what it means to be mini to her. I understand what's going on around me, but I don't yet have all the words in my tongue, that's why I talk out loud: so that the miracle will happen and those words not yet nested in my forked tongue will emerge like the fungus that grows out of the skin of the people who live near the Petroecuador refinery.

But my mami never talks about her fear; she tells me it worries her that I can't follow the thread of a conversation without tying on something else that has nothing to do with the first thing I was talking about. Like now, how I'm showing off my drawers and I start going on about my Mami Checho's fear of my loose tongue.

I don't know either why my ways of talking scatter, like when you piss out the window and you watch the drops cascade into a thousand threads in the dirt, sketching out a shape, like brown roots that later disappear with the force of the sun. That tiny moment when you can draw with the water that's born from your coochie is breathtaking. Although when my mami found me doing it, she asked do I think I'm a dog or what, and she almost smacked me against the window. But luckily my Papi Manuel, who laughs at everything, came in and calmed the waves.

In my little Riviel-spirit room I also have my bed; a

shoe stand where I put my rain boots, my tennis shoes, and my sandals; a nightstand with a lamp, which is really a yellow bulb held up by an animal that I can't recognize. Sometimes I think it's a cow, but its wings leave me stumped. I can't stand not knowing the names of things, so I named it Irene, and in my journal I wrote: *Irene is a porcelain animal that seems to be a mammal, but it has wings and an elephant's trunk.* My Mami Nela says it's the Devil and to throw that shit away. But I fall in love with everything around me, it doesn't talk to me from its throat but with its glimmer, twinkling like the parasites in a dog's wound, a cry that you don't hear with your ears but you feel in your whole body.

I love the light that comes in through the room's window and lights up the framed photos on the wall of my papi and mami when they were just married. Thick wooden frames with worn gold trimmings, in which they look grave and skinny, but also happier than I've ever seen them. At least my Mami Checho I haven't seen so happy since I was born.

There's also the photo from when I was little and they took me to see the Virgin of El Panecillo in Quito. I'm wearing a pair of black boots, which everyone hated but that me and my Papi Manuel loved, a furry green coat, a pink knit hat with a pom-pom, and my sea-bass grimace of a smile, grinning in the cold around the backside of the giant cement virgin. It's an instant photo, my Papi Manuel explained to me, they give it to you in just a few minutes, not like the Kodak rolls that you have to take to develop and many months can pass before you get to see your grin there in the plastic sleeves of the family photo album.

I also have a little round table that my Mami Checho calls my desk, to do my homework or sit and read, but I don't use it much. I do my homework in the dining room with my Ñaña Antonia, and I read my books up in the trees. I like to hear my voice through the noise that the wind makes in the guava leaves. My Mami Checho doesn't know that because she hates to see me perched up there like a sunning iguana, sweating like a pig. She doesn't understand that the trees call me with their subtle movements; they listen to me without fearing my tongue will stick in my throat. The trees are the only ones in this house that understand my raving.

My bed has a mattress that is hard but comfortable and helps me rest without my spine twisting. That's also why they take me to swim at the public pool, so my spine won't wiggle like a fumigated centipede and refuse to hold me up. I swim in my bed, I roll around, swimming among the pink sheets and the Simpsons coverlet. I breathe in deeply with my face pressed into the sheets, as if I were really diving into water, and I smell the odor of my piss.

I try everything I can to not piss the bed, but it keeps happening. The trembling in the bones of my face doesn't let me sleep. I close my eyes and hear the shot, and immediately the taste of the medicine they gave me mixes with my spit.

I can't sleep. I watch the movements of my trees through the gap I leave open in the window. They help me feel that I'm not making it up, that the story won't repeat. Like when I put a cassette on backward or rewind it, and the voices that were sweet and musical now sound like a million bees have slipped through the cracks in my head and are buzzing around inside me.

Awake, I think about the sounds of things and how the faces that enter my room in the darkness are no longer familiar and recognizable, but turn into hideous masses, and that's when without realizing it I start to piss myself, as if from the sky a hurricane has swept me up and I'm dreaming about a fight. I fall asleep and I piss myself completely.

My Mami Checho wants to pound me alive, to send me back to her belly, to eat me up with the mouth between her legs and disappear me into her insides, but I run away to the mango tree before she can catch me.

I don't know why I can't sleep. My Mami Checho

and my Papi Manuel explain to me that not all little girls get their own room, that I should take advantage of it, I should get enough rest. I don't know how to tell them that it's not me, that when I close my eyes in the faint light coming in through the window from the yard, the voices overwhelm me and the gunshot and the bodies of that night surround me in a clamor. But they can't understand that sometimes the words get hung up on my back molars, the ones I still haven't lost yet swallow them up and I can only shake my head mutely.

I know I'm lucky to have a little Riviel dugout room, but I can't make that night shut up. Every time the sun goes down behind the Guacharaca hill, the shadows return, like stray cats to Mami Nela's yard. I see the moving figures like scrawled outlines and my saliva turns bitter, becomes the nauseating potion, tasting of shit.

My bed starts to move, rocking back and forth, and the floor beneath my room is no longer wood, but now the brackish green water of the mangrove. Everything begins to sway, first to the right and then to the left. The bed teeters slowly, the window no longer lets in a faint light, but a brackish damp wind, the smut of the water. Like the drops that splash up as the motor of a fishing boat cuts decisively through the sea to bring fish, fruit, and humans from one island to another.

And out of nowhere the miracle happens and water is born from my coochie.

In the morning I'm wet and salty, as if I were emerging from the sea, not from a tranquil sleep. Noris washes the damp sheets and my Mami Nela brings me to her room to pray and to wash me. To explain to me that big girls don't piss themselves, carajo, how much longer with this wetting the bed, mamita. Mi amor, shame, what kind of example will you give your ñañita when she gets bigger if you're the bed-wetter?

In my room there's not only a desk, a dresser, a nightstand with Irene's house, and the bed that brings me to the sea. There's also a dressing table where I look at myself in the mirror and try to comb this untamable forest spirit that is my hair. I make little buns, all in a row with colored bands, I spray myself with my Little Women perfume, which quickly disappears, overshadowed by the stink from my underarms and my neck, I put pink lip gloss on my mouth, and I go out to play in the yard.

The sunlight invades my room and I feel it evicting me, like the sun and the wind are saying, excuse me, niña, we want to clean up this funk you've left here, go, go outside to the garden, get out of here. They send me out to wander like a lost soul, like an apparition, like the Tunda spirit in the bush imitating the voices of all the Black mamas:

Yuliana Ortiz Ruano

I'm the bed-wetter,
expelled from my room I walk through the garden
climb up the guava tree
to watch the light and the wind inhabit the space
where previously my body trembled.

I'm the bed-wetter,
I appear between the trees
talking to myself,
words without meaning,
neither heads nor tails,
or things with so many heads
impossible to find
the beginning
or the end
of the mouths alive in me.

I'm the bed-wetter,
I say strange things
that bring down the silence:
I say that once I saw shadows
in my Riviel dugout room
inside the plywood wall
I say that under those shadows
I made out

Carnaval Fever

my Papi Chelo's face
with a gun that exploded inside my body
a gun that burst me from the inside.

I say that the bullet
didn't enter my flesh,
didn't crush my intestines
but every night
it carries me back to that day.

Over and over again I buzz like a cassette
rewinding.

I'm the bed-wetter,
I don't know if the words
that lurch out of my mouth
teetering like an overweight fishing boat
are real
or are they an invention
of flesh and blood.

I'm the bed-wetter
and where am I going?
where the hell am I going?

And there's never any answer.

11.

Fever

I can't manage to figure out what's plaguing me. My memory is still a map hacked by machetes in the stinging, tentacled silence of the ñañerío and my Mami Nela. I've woken up with a fever ten out of every thirty or thirty-one days in the month.

The fever seems to breed in the depths of the backyard, outside my body.

It's true that my skin warms up, above all, my forehead, but this is an ancient fever, strange, that scurries up me like a scorpion before striking me with its sting. A fever hidden under layers of dirt, outside and deep down beneath the guava tree.

In my rainbow-colored bikini, my hair shoved into a rubber swim cap, I gaze at the sky-blue water. The reflection of the sky, also a heavenly blue, with clouds the color of pigeon shit, sways in this liquid universe that keeps me upright. My spine beat out a tattoo like a wriggling worm when they took me to get x-rayed, the day that I sat down to draw on the floor of the parlor and couldn't get up again.

Just what we needed! Mami Nela cried out, harassed, because it's true that my endless number of ailments and dramas already had them tearing their hair out. First the fevers, then the not sleeping, the talking to myself, and now my spine.

They plucked me up off the floor and took me in a taxi to Doctor Minda, who said that all I needed to do was swim regularly to get rid of the pain. That's why I started going to the public pool near the Las Palmas beach. Usually it's my Papi Manuel who takes me, though sometimes he just brings me in his truck to the Immaculate Heart of Mary school and then tells me to take the bus. Of course, I don't tell my Mami Nela and my Mami Checho that, because something about the way my Papi Manuel says it makes me understand that it's our secret. That I have to keep quiet.

On one of those buses, on my way to the pool, some old men started asking me why I was by myself. I said I was going to swim. I didn't want to answer, but sometimes the mouth answers, obedient. One of them, pointing his gaze between my legs, asked me if

I had menstruated yet. I answered no, moving from one side to the other my head turned to stone. Something massed in my throat and I wanted to run, but I stayed, tense. Another one of them told me, niña, don't wander around by yourself, little girls who wander around like that asking for it, and he stuck his middle finger in my mouth before he went running off.

It was the first time my trembling came on in the daytime. I arrived to the swimming class shivering and I was afraid of wearing my bikini in front of the teacher like I usually do.

When I changed in the dressing room, I stared fixedly at the outline of my coochie under the fabric. The power of feeling myself vaginated from just five minutes of staring made me tremble even more. I turned on the shower and held my face under the spray so I would stop twitching like a poisoned animal, I put my shorts back on over my swimsuit, and I went out to the class half clothed.

In the buses strange things always happen to me. Like what the ticket taker said about my ass and the way he looked at me, as if he could touch me with his fixed stare. But as soon as I climb up on the diving board and plunge into the sky-blue sheet of untouched pool, I completely forget the outside world, the buses, and the times I wait hours and hours for my

Papi Manuel until finally the teacher has to take me to the bus stop so I can catch the right one home.

The maladies started with the fevers. Sometimes I can even bring them on myself by breathing hard, without blinking, or they start with some suffocating dream. Then, when I'm boiling, I get up and go running through the house chattering, so fast my head doesn't know what's coming out of my mouth.

Sometimes I hear my Mami Checho insisting, cutting through the music they're playing at high volume, that I'm telling you, Manuel, if you keep on disappearing whenever you feel like it, I'm done with this shit once and for all. If he thought she didn't know that he looked for any excuse to take me to the pool to go after women and drink out in those neighborhoods. But my Papi Manuel always answers any complaint with a laugh, it's really useless to talk to him. As if instead of a tongue, he has a turntable deep in his throat playing the voice of La Lupe over and over again.

I must have learned it from this papi, my incurable chattering to the rhythm of son cubano, guaguancó and guaracha, with a vámonos pal monte, pal monte. That, I'm sure of.

The fever starts after dreaming the voice of La Lupe, that bloodcurdling laugh entering through my hair. First it comes whispering something real quiet, and then I manage to hear, from far off, that aayayayayayyy yiyiii-yiii gurrrrupi baby gurruuuupi, strangling me with the little bones under my neck. And then farther off, in the distance, the sobs of my Mami Checho and the animal laughter of my Papi Manuel, and then my fever positively spikes. In the morning, in the night, at every hour. This fever that isn't new, that started a long time ago.

My Mami Nela says that my fevers are from parasites and amoebas. She fixes a slice of lime, a bit of menthol, and a mix of macerated herbs, all in the little top of a Chinese menthol tin, and she places it on the burner to heat up. Then she grabs me between her legs, immobilizes me. She lets the mixture cool down a bit and then she pours the warm enema, burning, into my ass. Her index finger follows, its nail a wine red, into the depths of my existence, the furthest reaches of my void. I feel my body boiling inside and I can sense the beings who die to make me healthy. The beings who have to die, like in a war, like in the war with Peru over the Cenepa River, so that I can live.

But the fevers return like in La Lupe's song, expanding from the first feathery sound of trumpets, forming a hurricane, releasing in a voice that vibrates as if in fear, a fear of the Devil in her body.

The Devil only leaves me when I'm swimming or when I'm up in the trees.

How can I tell all these women that I've felt the Devil in my body, and more than once, in my little room that is also a body and as I'm the only one beating in it, I must be its heart.

I've felt a devil inside my room and sometimes I think it was only once, but I know that it's not the first time something has exploded inside my coochie.

How to form the words that mass in my throat into sounds, to fire them like bullets at the grown-ups, how to describe a song I love without using my mouth, how to explain to my schoolmates the screaming of La Lupe in the song about the fever.

Because only La Lupe can describe the birth of this fever, that turns the shadows into the Devil in my body, which she calls love, but which I can only identify as an enema pouring into my ass to save me.

I won't grow if I can't forget.

I think maybe I'll be trapped in this feverish body forever, with the pool fracturing my brain, the water pouring into the depths of my body like a balloon filled to burst in someone's face in Carnaval, as the swimming teacher yells at me to get out of the pool, that I can't hold my breath for so long, and I finally emerge, purple, like a terrible bloated mermaid. The teacher hauls me across the ropes dividing the swimming lanes and tosses my waterlogged body onto the floor.

The heads of the other kids in my swimming class wink into being under the heavenly blue sky, also trapped in the reflection of the pool. The kids stare at me, their hands over their mouths. I hear faint cries in the distance.

Up in the sky the birds are still flying.

Soon I catch my breath, I climb up the diving board, and I submerge myself again into the chlorinated womb that returns me to life.

I left a fetus in the lakes.
To tell the truth. I can impregnate myself.

Marosa di Giorgio, *Rosa mística*

12.

Sabrosura

Long before February it's already Carnaval in Esmeraldas, people soaking each other up in the houses, on the sidewalks, in all the parlors and bedrooms. My ñañas surprising each other with a soaking. If one of them has their back turned, washing the dishes and singing along to the salsa of the day or Mari Trini, another comes in with a bucket of water freshly brought up from the cistern to drench her. Toss that bucketful of water at her hair and start up running.

All the neighbors getting each other wet, dancing it all out on the sidewalk, shaking their asses and their hips as if they ruled over all the walks of life, as if their asses and their hips held up the world. Or is it that the hips and the asses only hold up this

Esmeraldeñan world of Carnaval salsa, madness, and raving?

I don't understand what the hell is happening in those bodies, in the neighbors out on the streets, the beach, and the city.

Just like I don't understand what the hell is happening in my cussed little body, heating and reheating; my body inflating and trembling, like the bubble of snot that escapes with the laugh of the little boy who lives across the street, whose family never bathes him. My body starts to boil all on its own, to fret, when January arrives and the inhabitants of this independent republic of flavor self-proclaim that it's Carnaval, and the calendar can't tell them a damn thing.

Doña Sabrosura was the one who said that thing about the independent republic. She's an old lady, but seems young. A lady so old, but also so sensual and full of joyful life that she seems more girlish than even this whole ñañerío.

Sabrosura sells casabe tortillas, banana preserves, sweet thick drinks of plantain or corn, dulce de leche, and other treats from a wooden cart mounted to a bicycle frame that I've never seen her ride. She's always dressed in white. She seems to appear out of nowhere, dragging her cart of casabes and mazamorras up to the corner of México and Cartagena, shouting: IT'S HERE, IT'S SABROSUUUUUUUUUUUURA.

And from all over, the packs of kids come running, desperate to lay hands on our own little tub of sweetness.

Sabrosura never wears shoes, but she always seems to have just washed. No matter how hard the sun beats down, she is sparkling, not a drop of sweat, her clothes a brilliant white, with her thick kanekalon braids and her laugh inundating the passageway of my Mami Nela's house. I go crazy for the taste of her drinks, her casabe, and her preserves, and I love it when she tells me, look, mija, you got to taste this: Carnaval is all flavor. You old enough to dance now, more'n what Jota taught you, may he rest in peace.

Ay, cuz these holidays coming up gon' be better than the past, mijita. The parties coming up always gon' be better than the past. Don't believe 'em when they tell you the past was sweeter; look here, mamita, before, we didn't even have 'lectricity, and now, mija, you see these hoods full up wit' speakers and the boys wit' their boom boxes, like money was handed out for free. What's goin' on in Carnaval I don't know, for these boys to be shitting out money, like the money's growin' up in them trees.

Sabrosura enjoys talking about Carnaval so much that when the holiday finally comes, she prefers not to go out at all, because the Carnaval coming up is always better than the last. Never see the party, only talk about it. Her tongue making its own jubilee. Her tongue brings its own speakers out to the curb, her tongue sets out the plastic chairs, fills them with lazy asses and hips, her tongue serves its own stew, a tapao arrecho to charge you up. I adore Sabrosura's chatter, a rumba of words and accents I don't fully understand.

Sabrosura always has something new to tell me: Word is that witch who live up on Aire Libre hill left her husband, and people seen her perched up there on the roof smoking pipe. Or, that old man who never let no one see in his cistern, what he have in there were money and drugs, mija, and the soldiers take him away. They nothin' but thieves theyselves, never trust them, ya hear? If sometime you got to travel out to that island alone, mija, and they call you down to inspect, say, NEVER LET GO YA BAG, MAMI, those soldiers plant drugs on fool little girls like you, so they can rape you and say you ask for it, some nasty shit, mamita, the north is in a bad way with all those soldiers.

To me, Sabrosura's smile is like a field of star coral, a whole beach of sand coating her throat as she cackles, shouting, PRESERVES, SWEETS, CASAAAAABE! IT'S HERE, IT'S SABROSURA.

Sabrosura sells nonstop in the months leading up to Carnaval. The months when everyone acts like the only way of life is throwing water in each other's faces, spraying beer out on the curb, and dancing wildly everywhere. Normally scarce in Esmeraldas, water suddenly multiplies infinitely, ready to attack, to savor and to tease, to cool the rumba's heat.

But in Carnaval people throw other things too. Once, my Mami Checho came home from work smelling of death because in the bus on the way home, someone had thrown their leftover water from selling fish on her. The bus passed right by the Stalls, where they say the slave market once was, but which now is like a kind of mall for selling fish and Colombian-made clothing. My mami arrived bawling that she was fed up with being treated like any old moron, over and over, almost crying: Manuel, we've got to keep on with the house, I'm going mad here, Jesus Christ. I have to get out of here, I can't stand the noise, the music... the unending rumba... I've had it up to here with these people.

My Papi Manuel and my ñañas reminded her that she's always lived here, surrounded by these people she detests. But she kept saying that she didn't know what was the matter, that she just wanted to be alone, to breathe, to be in silence for once in her life. And she shut herself into her room to cry for a whole day; she didn't even come out to eat.

Other times people throw beer, seawater, water mixed with egg, violently inflated colorful water balloons and hosefuls of water at people they don't even know, people who get real mad and sometimes fire shots into the air.

The gaggle of women in this house always reminds me never to throw water at anyone I don't know. I can stand on the curb with a bucket of water and throw it at the little neighbors, at the dogs, or at myself. Sometimes I go out to throw water balloons at the walls. I love the sound of the water running to the ground, the spluttering of the balloons bursting drowns me with pleasure. I laugh to myself, screeching, trying to imitate that sound.

Once when I was out bursting those colorful balloons against the walls of the house, a woman came down off her roof deck to ask me was I crazy or out of my mind or what. Didn't they teach me to be a normal little girl in my house? I just stared at her, not understanding, still splashing water on myself, bashing those balloons in blue, purple, red, against the ground. Mija, you don't play Carnaval by yourself, what's the matter with you? Go tell your mami to bring you to the doctor, you must be out of your mind, sick.

But I still like to throw water at the trees and the walls, because it's so hot. I can't imagine the suffering the skins of the houses must feel under the infernal sun of January and February. Under the humid rain that doesn't help at all with the inferno. You sweat even more when it rains; the earth turns into a boiling pot of tapao arrecho with us women swimming around in it like chunks of meat.

I never understand why older people insist that I play with other kids. They don't know that boys and girls only play at touching each other's coochies and weenies, and I don't like that. I want to keep eating dirt and guavas, talking to the plants and my ñañas, none of this awful little boys touching my body.

It's a lie, the happy gang of kids. What I see around me are a bunch of bloodthirsty midgets, disgusting little animals who stick their fingers in their asses and then make you lick them. I hate all the boys in my neighborhood and all the girls at school: they all just want to touch my coochie, climb up on me, lick my mouth like they're dogs or newly born rats. I don't want anyone to touch me, I just want to climb up in my guava tree forever.

That's why I prefer to play the fool up in the trees, talking with the noni fruits. The noni fruits stink, and that's why I feel they're like my siblings. I prefer to be up there in the stink of the noni tree than to play at papi and mami.

Even at my girls' school, we go to the bathroom together to see how some of us are starting to sprout hairs from our coochies. Of course, I never say *coochie* around my mamis and ñañas, they wouldn't like it at all. They hate bad words. But when I say them to myself I feel a tingling in my blood: *pussy, shit, ass, coochie*. Words that when spoken out loud draw an invisible knot in the air that can never be untied.

Sometimes my Papi Manuel hears me yelling at the noni fruits and he calls me down to ask if I'm ok, if I need anything. He says, Ainhoa, mija, come read with me, and he sits me down in the parlor to read any of the books that my Mami Checho has brought home from the library. Old books with the covers on backward or with pages ripped out, stuck in the library basement and forgotten about, like something worthless. My mami, who works there, circulating and registering all the books—but really more cleaning than circulating because almost no one ever goes—decided one day, these aren't going to stay down here rotting away, and she brought them home for me as a present.

In January, even the girls at my school all start throwing things at each other: tamarillo and orange juices fermenting in their dirty thermoses, the boiled egg and toast from their lunch boxes, water saved in empty glass jars. They're always talking about telenovelas, pop singers, things I don't understand because I don't get to watch TV. I go off to a corner of the classroom and I stand there staring at nothing with a fast trot rocking deep down inside my breastbone. It's as if we live on different planets. Me on a sickly earth full of dusty books, and them on a planet of screens and bright lights.

They ask me if I'm poor, if I don't have a television, if my parents are from the country, if I'm crazy. But to me, they're the crazy ones. I ask them if they know the names of the plants or the trees at their houses and they look at me with disgust, yell at me to get away, go over there by those books. Or go on, go talk to that plant way over there. And I run off, like an obedient dog, sit down away from everything and look at what they told me to look at. And then they laugh and I don't understand what the hell is happening.

Carnaval is the door opened to raving insanity, unending debauchery. As if someone has opened a faucet of partying that can't be closed, that gushes forth, overflowing any container. Adults stop taking care of kids. On the contrary. Once, I watched from my window as a bunch of kids heaved their drunk papi toward the Guacharaca hill.

One of the kids was crying, and all around grownups danced and grabbed each other's asses, nobody was helping them. I made sure that no one was watching, I put on my tennis shoes, and I went down to help the kids drag that papi along.

There were five of us, but all skinny and back-bent. The body weighed a ton, and it kept letting out horrible stanky farts, but I had pledged myself to the mission of rescuing this papi. I gave the little one who was crying a coconut cookie and told him not to worry, that my papi was also drunk, laid out on the sofa in my house, his snout open, and that papis are just like that. It's part of being a papi, getting drunk and falling asleep in impossible places.

In the end, two drunk women helped us to carry that loaded old man. As we went along, I tried to console the little one's crying. He was my same age, but seemingly it was the first time he had to help his drunk papi.

I was already used to seeing papis sleeping in the stairway, in the yard, on the toilet, in the bathtub, in the shower, in the car, on the sidewalk. Drunken papis just falling like ripe guavas all around us girls. When we could, we dragged them to their beds, and when we couldn't, we'd just cover them with a sheet and get out of there to go on with our lives.

I was not allowed to go up the Guacharaca hill. As my Mami Checho would say: STRICTLY FORBIDDEN TO SET ONE FOOT OUT THE HOUSE. But it was Carnaval and she was out in the backyard, dancing with her cousins who had come down from the north.

Checho doesn't even really like dancing, or listening to music, or drinking, or any of that nonsense, but Carnaval is for laughing, no need for crying, for having a good time. For enjoying, for singing, never for crying. Because "la vida es un carnaval," like the song says.

I just put my shoes on and took off, to help those kids mucking along with their drunk, fat papi; their farting, bare, drunk papi.

Totally bare and barfed on.

Maybe that's why the kid was crying, because it was his first time seeing his papi's private parts, or I dunno what he was thinking, poor thing.

We went up the hill until the pavement ended, and we kept going on up.

The two women stopped from time to time to rest and to hail the groups of dancers on every corner. To bum sips of whiskey or beer. The walk up the hill started to seem longer and longer and I felt dizzy because I had never walked up so high with people I didn't know. The dirt going up the hill was wet, but not quite mud yet. Even though you could clearly see the water rolling over and eddying around it, you could still walk without feeling the earth sucking you in.

In a natural science book, I read that every place is inhabited by different flora and fauna. Even though my Mami Checho had explained to me that us humans are not fauna, but humans, I looked at all the Carnaval rejoicing in my Mami Nela's house and all this heat and fever, fever and heat, as Grupo Saboreo says, on the walk up the hill, and I wondered if this way of being a human possessed by the Carnaval Devil is really a kind of fauna. And from the speakers of my Mami Nela's house, speakers throughout the narrow streets of the neighborhood, the voices chorused, telling that girl to scratch that itch, to grab her husband. What she needs is a man. That'll fix her arrechera.

Heat, fever. Fever, heat. Heat, fever, fever. Heat, heat. Fever, fever. Heat, fever. Fever, heat. Heat, fever. Fever, heat. Heat, fever, fever. Heat, heat. Fever, fever. Heat, fever. Fever, heat. Heat, fever. Fever, heat. Heat, fever. Fever, heat. Heat, fever, fever. Heat, heat. Fever, fever. Heat, fever. Fever, heat. Heat, fever. Fever, heat. Heat, fever. Fever, heat. Heat, fever, fever. Heat, heat. Fever, fever. Heat, fever. Fever, heat. Heat, fever. Fever, heat. Heat, fever. Fever, heat. Heat, fever, fever. Heat, heat. Fever, fever. Heat, fever. Fever, heat. Heat, fever. Fever, heat. Heat, fever. Fever, heat. Heat, fever, fever. Heat, heat. Fever, fever. Heat, fever. Fever, heat. Heat, fever. Fever, heat. Heat, fever. Fever, heat. Heat, fever, fever. Heat, heat. Fever, fever. Heat, fever. Fever, heat. Heat, fever. Fever, heat. Heat, fever. Fever, heat. Heat, fever, fever. Heat, heat.

Fever, fever. Heat, fever. Fever, heat. Heat, fever. Fever, heat. Heat, fever, fever. Heat, heat. Fever, fever. Heat, fever. Fever, heat.

Heading up the Guacharaca, I saw masses of people in a frenzied dance, all grabbing each other's asses, splashing whiskey into their traps as if an infinite cache had been unearthed in another secret cistern. All of this I had heard about from Sabrosura, but to see it up close, the Black fauna throbbing, moving all its abandon to the heat of the water and the steam rising from the earth, left me speechless. My mouth clean gone, like the dull bang and the smoke from a pistol fired by some kid up on a motorcycle.

The hill ended and just like that we went down the other side. We went up another hill, covered in groups of men and women dancing to songs that I had never heard in my life, songs they don't play on the radio at five in the afternoon, or in the morning, and by no means on a Saturday. Songs I had never heard from the speakers connected to my Papi Manuel's turntable. Songs I was completely ignorant of.

Songs even louder, snappier and with more swagger.

As if my head, too, were an old cassette player, one of those songs stayed burned into my memory forever. Most of all the jubilant faces crying out and the arms waving in the air, hailing the sky, eyes closed, singing to themselves. Maybe there was something religious in those lyrics, because the raised arms looked like the prayer circle women going off in an ecstasy during mass. Maybe it was a song to a God I hadn't met yet, I don't know, but that song nested in between my eyebrows forever. That schoolgirl so divine, the singer was dreaming, the singer was dying, he was going to teach her all about love.

There were also knots of boys in gold chains, beautiful Black boys wearing sunglasses just as black, pistols stuck into the waistbands of their loose white pants, dancing, chests bare. Some had bare feet, others, huge sneakers with neon stripes, unfurling their beauty in the dim light from the lampposts. As they drank in the street, they mixed with potbellied policemen, and the policemen, also drunk, fired shots into the air.

We arrived at the kids' house: a small wooden house with just one room, no walls or divisions, and two windows just like the ones you scribble in your notebook when you're learning to write. Up in the house, an impossible multitude of people danced to salsa and reggae, all of them wet, in the dark, speakers resting on the windowsills.

A huge woman came down, tall and really black, with blue eyes and silvery braids, and wearing a transparent white dress wet with sweat, beer, and whiskey. It seemed like she wasn't wearing any underwear, but I didn't look closely because I felt both embarrassed and like laughing, an involuntary gesture that my mouth kept making inexplicably throughout the journey over the hills. She tied a hammock between the pillars holding up the house in which everyone was dancing and stomping, tossed the naked drunk into it with one hand, and then told the kids to go to their grandmother's house to get something to eat and to sleep.

We said goodbye quickly, without even saying our names, and then I realized I didn't remember the way back home.

I stood there for a few seconds, staring at nothing, my mouth laughing without any command to do so, until I came round to a bucket of icy water flung in my face and I woke up all of a sudden.

I started to walk.

I walked down and up the hills I felt were the ones I had walked with those kids and their bare papi. I walked farther and farther into the crowds, feeling more lost all the time, more wet and more tired. I walked and asked for Calle México and Cartagena and the people laughed like mad in my face, as if what came out of my mouth had no place in their world.

A group of men in shirts made out of fishing nets, green, yellow, and red, threw cold beer on my head and my sleepiness vanished completely. Suddenly I recognized, like when you spy for the first time through a crack in the door your papi and mami making love, that I wasn't going to make it home by myself.

I kept going in circles, getting tangled up in groups of people more drunk and more frenzied. I saw a fat woman squatting down, two men putting their weenies into her mouth, a crooked lamppost tilting over them. It looked like not just the post but the whole world was about to fall on top of them, but they seemed to pay no heed to any of it. Maybe Carnaval is an animal that mounts you in your head and keeps you from thinking clearly.

I saw an old lady dancing, drunk, her breasts exposed: two purplish animals with lives of their own, round and full of flesh or mother's milk, strangling her neck as she poured over them an entire forty of beer, foaming, like a volcano exploding and dripping down between her big breasts. A man crouched under her soaking jugs, mouth open to the liquid cascading down, as if her breasts had now become a waterfall of life-giving milk.

I kept on walking. Eventually my feet started to hurt, so I took my sneakers off and went on. I stepped on dog and human shit, vomit, piss, also on two drunks laid out on the dirty ground and a broken bottle that buried itself in the sole of my right foot.

Limping, I went on searching for my house. I imagined myself lost forever, living in this overflowing, unending Carnaval for the rest of my life. I remembered that Sabrosura had told me never to walk alone uppathehill, that up there they rape little girls and say they ask for it, and what does that mean, rape, Sabrosura? I asked her. She just crossed herself, and then made the sign of the cross over my head and over the lower part of my body and I understood that rape was something bad for my coochie.

Just a few days before the frenzied explosion of partying, Sabrosura had suddenly looked at my neck, my belly, and my coochie under my shorts. She sucked in her breath, mamita linda, mi reina, mamita, mi vida, ay no, ay, Jesus Christ, ay, Jesus-Mary-and-Joseph, who's been hitting on my baby, mamita, ay no, God-and-the-Virgin no, mi vida, who's been getting up on you, mamita, ay no, mamita, please-Virgin, please-God, please-no, don't let it be true, by-the-Virgin, God-forbid, God-protect, grabbing my forehead in a frenzy. I couldn't even answer her because she just went off like a dog who's eaten poison, and when she saw my Mami Nela coming out of the passageway with a frown on her face, she ran off with her cart, yelling, CASAAAAAAAAAAAAAAABE, IT'S HERE, IT'S SABROSURA, crossing herself.

As if inside my head were a Bible, or a witch's fast-working prayer, just then a group of men on a corner yelled out, Rape!

Or at least, that's what I heard, in my unending desperation. I ran, the glass shards burying themselves even deeper in my foot. I was no longer myself but a panicked animal running for its life. I went on fast as the Tunda spirit, with her molinillo stick foot, a desperate lame maroon. I ran on, hoping to see mushrooming up by luck or by miracle down one of the streets behind the hill, my house and the ñañerío.

Rape.

Still I couldn't find my house. I imagined my Mami Checho drunker than I'd ever seen her, my ñañas drunk too, all crying for me in a festival of guilt.

An Esmeraldeñan guilt, to the tune of Los Van Van.

A boogielicious cry.

Piglike, frenzied, and foul smelling.

A rumba prayer in my name.
A grief to the beat of a drum.

I went along leaving tracks of blood over the vomit, the piss, the spilled beer: my own contribution to the shithole of Carnaval.

A man smoking an awfully stinky pipe called out to me, mami, come, have a try. I kept on going for a long, long time through colorful water balloons, buckets of icy water, frenetic dances, crazily swaying hips. Walking through bodies crawling along the ground and firing bullets into the air. Broken beer bottles, men and women screwing. Deafening music, undefinable smells: I was in the center of the straining heart of Carnaval.

13.

Whiskey

When I arrived back at the passageway of my Mami Nela's house, the sun was already lighting up the Guacharaca hill. The hill I had traveled, maybe even as far as the foothills of the Cerro Gatazo. My Mami Checho was asleep, her mouth hanging open, in bed next to my Papi Manuel. The ñañas were asleep too, some on the floor on woven mats or foam mattresses, all mixed up with cousins I didn't know. A long shoreline of open-mouthed women coming into life after the party.

Sitting near my snoring parents, one by one I picked all the glass shards from the soles of my feet. They were traced with a bloody map, faithful witness to my nighttime wandering. A monstrous map, built up with my secrets. I sprinkled what was left of a bottle of whiskey abandoned on the floor over the bloody holes in my feet and into my mouth, to feel that I was a part of the house. A dizziness among other dizziness. The galloping faded, like when you fall running and hit your head, hard. I sat there a minute, absorbing the senselessness with my tongue hanging out.

I made a space between the tired bodies of my Mami Checho and my Papi Manuel, folded their arms over my body, and fell asleep.

The Carnaval beat finally turned off.

14.

Mama Doma

I'm a little seed of living water tucked in among the layers of my ñañas and my mamis.

Like the most intimate heart of the onion. Deep inside all the thick, fat rinds, the flesh of my existence.

I'm starting to get fed up with it.

Something tells me I've been in some sort of danger and that this gaggle of women has saved me, but I'm not so sure. Before Carnaval, before losing myself on the hill, I promised myself that I would start to keep my own secrets. An innermost, unnamed fruit I guard jealously so I can feel that I have my own life. That I'm not just the center of all these layers of women who've saved me from something I can't grasp. A something that starts growing in the center of my body, like a small watermelon, broadening just to the left of the mouth of my stomach and descending slowly to concentrate in a throb just above my coochie.

My ñañas and mamis have decided, certain things are not allowed into my head. So I'm keeping their heads out of this new inner reserve; it's only fair. You can't keep opening your trap to try to say what you feel and what's happening to you and get nothing in return.

As this seed-bubble of air grows inside my body, so does my little sister, slowly, and so does my Papi Manuel and my Mami Checho's longed-for house. The house that for now is just an empty lot populated by ungovernable weeds in the middle of the countryside. Far from the noise and the ignorant rumba that my Mami Checho hates, that overwhelms her head.

My ñañita is growing slowly and I am turning into a woman: a premature woman, an inwardmotherñaña. Where the faces of my Papi Manuel and my Mami Checho should be inside my head, I have to draw my own face. A madrecita broadening like a filling water balloon, ready to burst against some wall or in the eye of a dumb passerby in Carnaval.

I keep broadening. I'm afraid of leaving this house, this garden, where my umbilical cord is buried, and my hairs, my nail cuttings, my piss, my love letters to the trees, and the questions that won't come out of my mouth, but seem to flow out all by themselves in my journals. Why does my body throb so much? Why does my coochie hurt when I piss? Why is my body inflating with breath and thick slime?

I am terrified of leaving my ñañas alone. Papi Chelo's presence threatens to return at any moment, like a flesh-and-blood ghost, to eat up their bodies and their smiles. When I think about this next age, the age of becoming a woman, of growing in height, of sprouting an ass and rounding curves, my head goes up in flames. I don't want a curvy body. I would rather concentrate on the throbbing urgency to turn myself into my guava tree, or the ice-cream-bean tree in Remberto's yard. To grow, unbothered, peaceful, toward the depths of the sun.

There are things I can't say out loud, like my age or my name, or the name of my sister. Noris and I are responsible for her now. The ñañas have had to go out to work, to throw themselves against the world, like a fisherman's eye clouding over under the sick heat of the sun. The radio doesn't play the same music anymore at five in the afternoon; the rumba of the neighborhood has been switched off, like a candle left for a saint in a poor neighborhood church, snuffed abruptly. On the radio there's only talking: of banks gone bust, money disappeared, aid funds, things I don't understand, but they make a mess of my head.

In my house nobody has time to play with me anymore, because there's no money now for dumb costumes and all that damn nonsense.

On the radio, the new song is crisis.

Up the street and down, ever since I was born the word *crisis* has been growing from under my neck, bulging like a jigger sore. Like this invisible swelling that won't let me breathe.

I hold in my hands the pale face of my ñaña attached to her almost-baby body, the body of a baby who's almost not a baby any longer, and I feel like crying.

I rock her as I sing a beautiful song I heard at a wake a long time ago, a song that helped us all to cry, that made me piss out of my eyes as if I had really known the dead guy. I whisper softly so as to not arouse in her an urge to dance, because I want her to go to sleep. At least for a couple of months. Until my body calms down and I can discover just who is responsible for this cry boiling in a pot in my chest since I was born.

I keep rocking and rocking my little sister. She's so beautiful, like an apparition of the Virgin, descending, pale, from the heads of the people imagining her. Like God and the Devil in the land of the sun that falls unconscious behind the Guacharaca hill.

I know plenty that being too beautiful is no good. My head still carries the ugly things that happened to my Ñaña Rita, just for having a face marked with beauty.

And again the pot of cries overflows and I suck them down, like a nasty stew.

I say softly, God, dear God, if you exist, watch over my ñañita, keep her safe from the neighborhood boys.

Keep her safe so no one will tell her how delicious her ass is when she goes out without me.

I repeat: God, dear God, if you exist, keep this little girl safe from the hands of men who go into rooms when you're sleeping and then you don't understand why your head and your coochie hurt and you feel like crying all the time. I say: dear God, if you're here among us, as my Mami Nela says, please take care of my ñañita. Stick my hand to hers forever, so that nobody can enter her room while she's sleeping, so that I can always be there, so I can understand why my body hurts and I feel like crying, but my mouth closes up like the black mussels harvested by women in the mangroves.

I tell Noris to lay her down in her crib, which is almost too small for her, because my ñañita is growing vigorously, like the bush growing up around the trees, slowly but surely, powerfully.

I go to the window of my room, from where I heard the shot or the noise that night Papi Chelo came in with his stench of grain alcohol. A noise that reached my head like an army of manta rays, wings outstretched, and everything was wrecked, like a sick animal's diarrhea spilled out on the floor.

My head is a motorboat with me aboard, trembling as I cross the yard, while these manta rays launch their aquatic flight between the salt water and the daylight dropping down behind the Guacharaca hill.

I think: anywhere could be a shore, this yard could be a shore.

I see myself walking on the imaginary seawater, like my Mami Nela told me Jesus was said to walk.

Every time my Mami Nela tells me about Jesus, I want to ask, why don't we pray to Mama Doma instead? Mama Doma, who saved people with her herbs, who helped women give birth when they didn't have money for the clinics where the white women or the rich Black women go.

Mama Doma, who saved people who are still here with us.

Jesus, I don't know if he really walked on that water or saved all those people, but Mama Doma I do know from the mouth of my Mami Checho and the hundreds of mouths who speak her name through these streets. A tree of mouths, beaming to the beat of Mama Doma.

There's always someone coming by from the north or from Colombia to bring us a bunch of salted fish or crabs, or fruit or plantains, giving thanks and crying because Mama Doma had cured them of some illness. Had returned them to life, like a god of herbs and potions.

Why do we cry out in prayer to Jesus, and not to Mama Doma, who is ours? She who is truly the vagina from which we all emerged.

That's it.

I run out to the backyard, I kneel between the two trees, under which are buried my umbilical cord, my hair, and my nails. I plant my knees there, but I don't put my hands together, I place them on my belly, which begins to boil harder. I don't look to the heavens; I'm sure that Mama Doma is scattered among the earth, or perhaps she is born again, she has sprouted from a piece of earth to live among us.

And I begin to pray:

        Mama Doma,
you who exist
you who are the truth
like the sleeping plants
living silent lives in the garden
like the clouds passing slowly over the hills
like the thick voice coming out of my throat
like the cries and the pain
from your daughters' bodies

        Mama Doma,
you who are absolute
like the holy water I secretly drink
to cure my tears
like the horse whip that breaks my ñañas' skin
the girls' skin,
everyone's skin,

        Mama Doma,
you who are the only sure thing in this house

Carnaval Fever

help us

may the music return to our neighborhood
the mouthful of slugs on the radio
at five in the afternoon
may my ñañas laugh and play again

leave off working for rich folks
leave off being poor

may my little sister grow free of hands
free of faces appearing beneath sheets

may my ñañita grow healthy
with my hand in hers
my hand on her body
may the hands of the neighborhood men
never blanket her body

may her body never feel this burning,
confusing heat
may she know who is covering her mouth
touching her legs
as she decides that it's all a bad dream
that nothing is certain

Yuliana Ortiz Ruano

may my cry wither
like the rivers polluted with oil
like the skin of the people who burned to death
when the city flooded with oil

Mama Doma,
help me be wise like the plants
silent as the noni bushes
generous as this guava tree
expansive as Remberto's ice-cream-bean tree

Mama Doma,
you who are the truth
you who never looked on my face
nor I on yours
but my hands remember your paths
scattered throughout my memories,
make this garden
and this house
our home again.

I grab a chunk of dirt and stuff it in my mouth. I chew it and hold it in, and my saliva starts to flow like a river. With my tongue and my teeth full of dirt I think: let it be so.
Mama Doma, let it be so.

15.

Whales

Everything in my head is the murky water of a contaminated river. My brain churns and sloshes from one side to the other within the bones that contain it.

I dreamed that my brain dripped out through my nose, like pink boogers, like a kid vomiting up a kilo of cotton candy from the fair out by the river. My brain spills out of my skull, it weighs so much I can't get out of bed. The grown-ups don't understand that when a girl's brain turns to Jell-O, or bubble gum, she should have the right to just be left alone.

To be left to sleep, to turn into pink tripe and flake away. These women do just the opposite. They haul me up out of bed and stick me up any old place. My body flakes off throughout the house, leaving bits of me on the sheets, my sandals, my school uniform, in the bathroom. I'm nauseous all the time. I wish my brain would vomit out my mouth once and for all so I can stop thinking about it turning into a thick, noxious slime.

When a girl's brain turns to mush, not only does her body boil like a plantain dumpling soup, enough to burn up a whole town if it spilled over, but also her thoughts inside shimmy a murderous dance, destroying her. Everything this girl thinks turns into a clot of blood rolling slowly along the floor of the house.

My brain is a stray blood clot and school doesn't help one bit. There are empty chairs, girls who arrive their hair a mess, dirty and with sleepers in their eyes, or slurping up their snot because their papis just said goodbye, they're going off to Spain. Girls who don't come to class anymore because their mothers took them away to Europe: Spain, or maybe Switzerland. Other girls with stories about their mamis going to Atacames to look for a gringo husband, or saying, my mami told me that when I get older she's going to take me to Same, because a lot of gringos visit the beach there.

What does that mean, that your mami is going to take you to Same to see gringos?

Is there a special place you go to see gringos, like whales? I imagine the beach at Same full of bodies, little balls of human meat spilled everywhere, as the mamis point out to their daughters with binoculars the heaps of gringos just arrived in this little country trembling with the word *crisis*, like a constant whistle coming from the radio. Day and night, crisis is the new rumba dancing on the radio.

Crisis and on the radio stories of the motorboats fleeing, Ecuadorian migrants packed in like sardines, disappearing forever across the dull gray sea in the direction of the United States. Crisis and a mob of Ecuadorians walking across the Guatemalan border to cross into the United States. Crisis and the kids across the street never bathed, never watched over, as my Mami Nela says, just up and abandoned by their papi and mami, gone to Chile or maybe the United States.

Crisis.

Crisis.

Crisis.

Bank holiday, but here there is neither holiday nor happiness, only death on the radio. People jumping from buildings in Guayaquil, a mob of people taking to the streets, the only pressure valve there is.

My brain is a blood clot and the streets don't help either: There are lines for buying milk, lines for buying bread, lines outside the banks. Tears outside the banks, people burning tires outside the banks, flaming tires inside the banks. My Papi Manuel and my Mami Checho put on their baggy jeans, red handkerchiefs over their faces, and go out to burn tires too. To burn garbage and break up pieces of curb to throw at the banks and at the police.

The streets are a photograph burning up for good.

Sometimes I go with them, and I raise my fists without really knowing what's going on. But this time I'm not that bothered that I don't really understand the devastating effects of the word *crisis* coming out of the radio. It seems there isn't time to sit down and really talk about what's happened, but I'm part of the group, of the shouting, of the fighting: that's enough for me.

My brain is a blood clot and it doesn't help that my Mami Checho's friends come by to convince her once and for all to go find work in Madrid. Without my Mami Checho everything would fall apart. My Papi Manuel first of all; his head rolling desperately all down Calle México, his head decorating the city in flames, his head feeding the buzzards who've come downtown to eat the garbage. I can't imagine my life without my Mami Checho. I think about her leaving and I can't stop the shaking.

My brain is a blood clot and it doesn't help that my ñañas are all gone now, off working. My ñañas get home tired and there are no more games, no dressing up as witches, no reading in the hammock, no dolls, no more voices of Chilean and Spanish divas coming from the radio. My ñañas have grown up and I don't know how to navigate this house without their hands at every turn.

To grow up is to churn your brain in a blender of bones called your skull.

One Saturday morning during these confusing days my Papi Manuel took us whale watching. I was pleased the whale watching happens in September, because it's also my birthday, and to me, the whales coming that same month to the shore of my house was anyhow a goddamn gift. My Papi Manuel sold his old truck to a newly arrived Arab who opened a restaurant on the beach. He came by with an old mechanic from La Boca del Lobo neighborhood and bought it for a few dollars. This new way we have to shape our food and our lives. Our existence now measured by the dollar.

It was the first time I saw my Papi Manuel really cry, hiccupping and suffocating himself desperately in the sofa in my Mami Nela's house. The crying of papis and mamis is like a melody that sticks in your chest, anchoring you like a motorboat to the dock of an island with no map. A sound that breaks your bones and brings your papis and mamis to dwell among the broken bits forever.

My Papi Manuel bought an awful car, an old brown Lada also with a sick noise. It seems like a scandalous sob always follows him, but it works to bring him, my Mami Checho, my ñañita, and me around the city and to the beach. He bought it grudgingly from a coworker who sold everything, even his job in the electric company, to go eat shit in Madrid. My Papi Manuel said to him, when he came by my Mami Nela's house to leave the car, man, be serious, how you gonna be such a bonehead, you got a good job here and you're gonna go clean shit for those goddamnsonsofbitches? The man took the green bills from my papi with desperation and put them into his wallet in the right-hand pocket of his pants. We never saw him again.

One Saturday morning we all went up into the hills to the south, toward the beaches that belong to the pampered Quito families. Not that those beaches are in Quito; on the contrary, they're on our own same coast. But when you get there, you don't feel at home. All around are different accents and creamy red bodies, like the monstrous boys from the capital.

We parked the car by the Súa boardwalk, on a long street full of shops selling beachwear: sky-blue and white bikinis, fake straw hats, and sarongs decorated with palm trees and sunsets. The beach at Súa that day had a beautiful greenish tinge and the sun brought out the subtle variation between the sea and the arm of fresh water that empties onto the beach. We boarded a fishing boat. The boater asked me if I was afraid, but, offended, I yelled back at him: what's the matter with you? I was born up in a boat, I'm from Limones I am. My Papi Manuel and the boater fell all over themselves laughing, but my Mami Checho shot me an angry look. She's determined to make me into a little woman and little women don't answer back like that. I should have laughed dumbly and shut my trap, but no, there I was hotly mouthing off about my lack of fear.

I moved up to the tip of the boat, as little by little it started to roar, gathering speed, killing time for a few minutes in the search for a whale. Before we started out, I looked at my unstable reflection in the green water of Súa and I asked myself, what is that there in the water, is it a mini-woman or what? Am I or am I not a woman trembling, like a shiny capsule of vitamin E, reflected in the greenness of the salty water?

I breathed in and out.

Above my coochie something boiled; I could have sworn a cluster of life swelled there, a non-organ taking on my breathing, taking my vital signs and making them theirs, for the rest of my life. Something beating like the heart of a small animal. I could sense the veins bringing blood from the emptiness in my belly to explode two fingers below my throat. Up in the boat my body, without asking me, took off and jumped into the water.

Quickly salt invaded my head, my nose, and my girl-not-woman body. With my eyes closed, I felt my blood and bones transforming themselves into manta rays, unbothered, moving their cartilaginous wings through the water. Moving my body in a slow flight, draining my life away.

While I drowned I thought about the encyclopedias of maps and marine animals that my mami had brought home from the library months ago. I felt myself plunging into the greenness of the sea, painted a flat sky blue on all the maps. Underneath anything that's painted just one color is some bit of a lie, even the encyclopedias with their sky-blue-seas lie. I let the water pour into me. Maybe the seawater holds the possibility to become cartilage and flight, to stop living daily in the rubbery thoughts that make me want to vomit.

The water was flowing into the cornucopias of my nose, melding with my brain, when I saw the fishlike shadow of my Papi Manuel approaching slowly, as if the force of his plunge were birthing him into the body of the sea. He came swimming toward me with a strange grimace on his face, as if saying, not yet, mija, it's not time to leave us yet, the flight under the sea is only after you're done being a girl. As if saying, mija don't be such a bonehead, come on, missy, you're not ready to return to the sea, mamita. Mamita bella, what's the matter with you, where you think you going?

He grabbed my body in his skinny arms and hoisted me up so that the boater could pull me up again, could bring me back into the air.

My Mami Checho was crying, holding my ñañita, begging to go back to shore. I said that I wanted to see the whales, that I felt better after my bath. My papi and the boater roared again with laughter, but my mami's anger blanketed the waves.

Finally we headed out to open sea to see the whales up close.

Don Oscar, the boater, told us that every year the whales come to mate off our coasts. That the jumping of the whales is really a kind of courtship. Like when, as a man, you dance wit' the bitch you fancy, you know? he said, looking at my papi. My mami told him to please watch his language there, friend, because we've got babies here. Then the boater shoved his tongue up his ass and didn't say no more.

We all stayed quiet, waiting for the whales' miraculous flight, but nothing happened.

My ñañita got seasick and threw up formula and

Cerelac into the cloth diaper on my mother's left shoulder. Seeing no animals in flight, other than the same seagulls as always, Don Oscar gave a few sharp pulls to the Yamaha motor to return us to shore when it happened. The whale breached only a few meters away from our motorboat. We saw her leap, like a giant basketball player shot bang in the head while trying to make a basket.

And just like that, as if letting herself be taken by the wind, she started her joyful return to the water.

The boat swayed from side to side and we had to hold on tight so as not to fall in along with the queen whale, who had allowed us to witness her. For the first time I felt that the prayers I'd made to Mama Doma were taking effect. The same whale, or perhaps another, returned to lift herself up over the dazzling green horizon of Súa in the sun. The beauty of its enormous body made me think again about jumping into the sea, about turning into an aquatic animal, calming the new throb settled in my insides. I could have sworn I'd grown a heart in there above my coochie. I'd dreamed my flaming body falling from the top of the Cerro Gatazo, my brain turned into mashed potatoes and my girl's body rolling along, letting myself be rolled up in something to be broken. That's it.

My girl-not-bitch's body needed to set out over the waves, violently. Like the jump of a whale driven mad by the urge to catch his mate. I wanted that thrust, to lift up a heavy body as easily as flipping a pancake in a Teflon pan.

To lift up these kilos of life and burst back into the salty semigreen mass of the sea.

I needed to break out of my head, get out of the creamy paste nestled inside the bones above my neck. My skull, a transparent sack of slimy water. My skull full of bloody clots and rotting scorpions soaked in the cerebral paste, making it hard to breathe and beating in my chest. The whales kept breaching and lowing like cows in the water. I wanted to cry from joy, but what I really needed was that body, that ability to raise myself up and bash myself against the salty water. That's it.

I quickly ran up to the tip of the boat and jumped back into the water.

16.

Flor de verano

Vi navegar una flor
una flor en el verano

I watched a flower sail on by
a flower of the summer
across the sea all you could hear
was its beautiful aria
it sang a song so mysterious
that the waves carried with them
era un canto misterioso
que las ola'iban llevando

cuando se pierde un amor
el amor que uno más quiere

Yuliana Ortiz Ruano

>if your love is lost
>the most beloved of them all
>se desgarra el corazón
>se desgarra el corazón
>y se le hacen mil pedazos
>your heart is torn to shreds
>your heart is torn to shreds
>into thousands of pieces
>the sky fills with dark clouds
>but they never stay for long
>through a crack in the heavens
>appear feathery white ones
>and that's what love is
>when it's lost and it's ended
>y así mismo es el amor
>y así mismo es el amor
>cuando se pierde y se acaba
>y así mismo es el amor
>y así mismo es el amor
>cuando se pierde y se acaba
>y así mismo es el amor
>y así mismo es el amor
>cuando se pierde y se acaba

The voices chorus around me, chanting again and again. Their breath stirs around me, from front to back, from right to left. Their hoarse, jangling voices ripple in circles, rocking me like a vivid sun-induced dream, a never-ending delirium. Within the sound are little hiccups, like grains of rice, or like the coffee beans sprinkled out to dry along the edge of the asphalt highway. Grainy voices gyrating again and again around my body, still as a newly born puppy.

> the sky fills with dark clouds
> but they never stay for long
> through a crack in the heavens
> appear feathery white ones
> and that's what love is
> when it's lost and it's ended
> y así mismo es el amor
> y así mismo es el amor
> cuando se pierde y se acaba
> y así mismo es el amor
> y así mismo es el amor
> cuando se pierde y se acaba

Anywhere could be a shore, anything can expand into the rocking of a canoe fixed to a lost pier, a pier swaying far from any human eye, no hip to be jarred up in the boat by the smack of the tide. This must be how it feels to die: the rocking of a watery hammock dragging out your cry, the beating in your throat, and the throbbing in your belly. A coming and going heard not with the ear, but through some invisible opening connecting the bodies softly crooning a goodbye to life and a welcome to death. Submerging your head in the water and hearing, from far off, someone singing your name: an Ainhoooaaa fragmented with bubbles of air, grainy disruptions in the singing voices.

Little by little I start to pick out faces in this blinding light. A new whiteness inhabiting my horse eyes. A milky dawn formed out of heaps of leaves and clouds, with just a pinch of whistling breeze. I can sense their closeness, joined to me by a meaty muscle that's impossible to touch. My Mami Checho's head, hair covered with a nylon stocking; my Ñaña Antonia, turbaned with a red rag; the braided head of my Ñaña Tita; Noris's balding head; and the silvered kanekalon braids decorated with cowry shells hanging down Sabrosura's neck.

I know that we are in my Mami Nela's garden because, even through the whiteness and the lightning flashing in my eyes, I can see my guava tree behind the heads. A few hanging fruits send far-off greetings, greenings, wishing me luck. I want to move, to stretch out, to understand this commencement of my wake in the yard, but I can't. Under my body a blanket insulates me from feeling the earth directly, but still, the little stones and bugs creep over me, touch my skin, announcing their presence. I open my mouth and what comes out is a vapor that refuses to bite down on the sound of the word. I make an effort to sit up, but I can only feel above my neck, my body won't listen to reason.

I lick my lips with a dry tongue and on the upper one I taste drops of bitter sweat. A horse has fallen, a horse has entirely broken down inside my head.

Sabrosura squats down as if she's coming in from another dimension, a slow movement that overwhelms me with vertigo. Now that all the bodies and voices move with this new slowness, I can better see how Sabrosura's face is like a pot of her own dulce de leche set out in the sun, shining, lustrous, free of sweat or blemishes. Her dark palm-seed eyes coming in from beyond the earth and her voice a purple like the mussel shells, grating out a stay still, mamita, don't you get up yet, mija, it's early still, it's early, mamita, mi dios, ay, mi mamita, mi dios.

Her voice filters slowly into my mouth, and I no longer feel the throbbing life within my life. Behind her a brown tub and a haze of smoke, and I can see a sprig of chamomile burning. Below my navel, little by little, second by second, a swelling is born. Something swells between my legs. I want to draw myself a pair of eyes two fingers below my coochie to see this leaking up close. I cough out a white froth from my mouth that tastes of spit, orange, and the faint memory of a grain alcohol cure. A liquid fullness continues to push through, lowering second by second between my legs. A tiny throb expands also in my chest, beneath the cage of bones protecting my stopped heart. Lowering, descending, and I realize that if I was born from a water-mami, then I must be more water than stink, more water than body of flesh. I drain away, gasping like a carp plucked from the water, still slimy, eyes and skin filming over.

Inside the water that won't stop flowing, my body is a sheet of glass, a glass balloon held by a pair of loose threads. I could swear that today the life inside of me is falling out, my coochie is falling out, and I panic because I know that's the only thing my Mami Checho didn't learn to heal, the only thing that was left unfinished from what Mama Doma taught her. My Chechito only knows the names of the herbs, but not how to cook them, how to mash them, she doesn't know if she has to give them in a tonic or massage them herself, with her librarian-cleaning-lady hands, directly on the fallen coochie. Now the water flows out not only below me but also from my eyes, the rivers inside me escape, trembling, and I cry out. I'm screaming inside and I hear, from far away, the cries of my Mami Checho, snotting and leaking, crying, mija, ay, mija, dios, why did you allow this, God, why my little one, mi dios, why do you allow this.

But her cries are muffled in the heads joining around me, in the hand of Sabrosura that stitches to my hand as if our skin had no border. The painful draining away makes me imagine the flesh and the water of my ñañas and Sabrosura as one flesh, like modeling clay mixing and melting its colors together into one big mass, powerful and pure. A river dries up between my legs. Down below a scab hardens out of what was the water between my legs and now feels like rubber cement gluing my thighs together.

Around me the colors of everything burn, the guava tree burns, my legs catch fire from this infinite piss that I can't even see up close because I can barely breathe and I'm draining away through my eyes. It's hot, I'm sweating, but from my wrists to my fingertips everything is icy cold. Surely if my hands had teeth they would be chattering like a couple of never-ending biting machines.

I'm draining away,
I'm swaying within.
This must be how it feels to die.

The heads sobbing, but still singing.

Song list

"Fiebre," La Lupe (Latin soul, Discuba, 1988)
"Aquí el que baila gana," Juan Formell, Los Van Van (timba, composed by Juan Formell, Planet Records, 2007)
"La suegra voladora," El Sayayín (champeta, composed by Jhon Jairo Sayas, Rocha Disc S.A.S, 2001)
"La vamo a tumbar," Grupo Saboreo (currulao, composed by Octavio Panesso, Alos Producciones, 2000)
"Cuerpo a cuerpo," Grupo Cariaco (tropical, Discos Fuentes, 1989)
"Olvídame y pega la vuelta," Pimpinela (ballad, composed by Lucia Galán, Joaquín Galán, Sony Music Entertainment Argentina S.A., 1982. In Ecuador, the disk was released in 1983 by CBS.)
"Fruit de la passion," Francky Vincent (zouk, Arcade Records, 1991)
"Anda ven y quiéreme," Juan Formell, Los Van Van (timba, salsa, composed by Juan Formell, Unicornio Producciones Abdala, 2004)

Song list

"Préstame tu mujer," Ray Barretto (salsa, guaguancó, Fania Records, 1984)

"Qué lío," Hector Lavoe and Willie Colón (salsa, composed by Willy Colón, Héctor Lavoe, and Joe Cuba, Fania Records, 1972)

"San Martín ha llegao," traditional arrullo to San Martín from the island Limones, Esmeraldas, Ecuador

"Manteca de iguana," traditional Colombian children's song

"El llorón," Ledesma (dembow, 1998)

"5 de septiembre," Vico C

"Vámonos pa'l monte," Eddie Palmieri

"Con el Diablo en el cuerpo," La Lupe (Latin soul, Discuba, 1988)

"La vida es un carnaval," Celia Cruz (salsa, composed by Víctor Daniel, produced by Isidro Infante, RMM Records & Video, 1998)

"La arrechera," Grupo Saboreo (currulao, composed by Octavio Panesso, Alos Producciones, 2000)

"Colegiala," Jorge Leo and Atrato River (salsa, composed by Jorge Leo Mena, Discos Dago, 1995)

"Flor de verano," traditional arrullo (recorded by Papá Roncón and Katanga with Catalina Quintero, Oriente Music, 2003)

Yuliana Ortiz Ruano was born in 1992 in Esmeraldas, Ecuador, and is an Afro music DJ, a novelist, and a poet. She is the author of the collections *Sovoz*, *Canciones desde el fin del mundo*, and *Cuaderno del imposible retorno a Pangea*. *Carnaval Fever* won the Joaquín Gallegos Lara National Fiction Prize, the Primo Romanzo Latinoamericano Award, and the PEN Presents English PEN award.

Madeleine Arenivar is a literary translator from Spanish living in Quito. Her translations of short fiction have been published in *Another Chicago Magazine*, *Latin American Literature Today*, and *The Los Angeles Review*. Her work has been selected for a PEN Translates grant, the PEN Presents program, and the *Best Literary Translations* anthology. *Carnaval Fever* is her first book-length translation.